TOPZ SECRET DIARIES

DAVE'S DIZZY DOODLES

Alexa Tewkesbury

CWR

What's up, peoples? It's me, **Dave the Rave** – the first one in the Topz Gang to become a Christian! When you ask Jesus to come into your life, you don't need to be anywhere special. You can be inside, outside, upstairs, downstairs. I was in my bedroom. Awesome, huh?

Things have been a bit weird lately. I'm usually the sensible one, the one who helps the other Topzies when they get themselves into a muddle – which they do quite often because they're kind of a crazy bunch! If you don't already know about us you can find out who we are on the next page. But this time it's been me who's needed a helping hand. You see, sometimes how you feel can take you by surprise – and if it's a bad feeling, you need to give it to God straight away, otherwise it can grow and grow and lead to all sorts of trouble.

But what I've been finding out is that with God, it's never too late. He's always right there waiting for us to come to Him.

Itching to know more? It's all here – so get on and get reading!

HI! WE'RE THE TOPZ GANG

– Topz because we all live at the 'top' of something …
either in houses at the top of the hill, at the top of the
flats by the park, even sleeping in a top bunk counts!
We are all Christians, and we go to Holly Hill School.

We love Jesus, and try to work out our faith in God
in everything we do – at home, at school and with our
friends. That even means trying to show God's love to
the Dixons Gang who tend to be bullies, and can be a
real pain!

If you'd like to know more about us, visit our website
at **www.cwr.org.uk/topz** You can read all about us,
and how you can get to know and understand the Bible
more by reading our 'Topz' notes, which are great fun,
and written every two months just for you!

SATURDAY 5 AUGUST
3.15pm

Benny rang. He said, 'Sorry, but I can't come over. Mum says I've got to tidy my room.'

I said, 'Can't you tidy it tomorrow?'

He said, 'That's what I said to Mum.'

I said, 'What did she say?'

He said, 'Well, "No", obviously.'

I said, 'What's the rush?'

He said, 'We've suddenly got this boy from France coming to stay.'

'What boy?'

'Kind of like a cousin, Mum says.'

I said, 'Didn't you just have a cousin to stay a little while ago?'

'Well, yeah, but that was Jake,' Benny said. 'Jake's my real cousin and he's really small. This boy from France is the same age as us. He's the son of Mum's best friend from school, which sort of makes her like an auntie, Mum says. That's what I call her anyway. Auntie Jess. So that's kind of what makes him like a cousin. Mum says we've all met before but I was only little so probably won't remember … which I don't.'

'So,' I said, 'you've got some boy from France coming to stay who you don't remember but is kind of like a cousin because his mum is kind of like your auntie … only not?'

'Yup,' said Benny, 'that's about it.'

'Why?'

'Mum says it's to help out. Auntie Jess isn't very well. She's been in hospital having operations and needs to rest a lot.'

'Oh,' I said. 'When's he coming?'

'Tuesday,' Benny said.

'Oh. How long's he staying?'

'Dunno. Don't think Mum knows.'

'Oh. What's he called then, this boy?'

'Thomas.'

'Oh … triffic.'

3.25pm

Benny rang. He said,

'Done it!'

I said, 'Done what?'

He said, 'My room. So I'm coming round.'

I said, 'Cool. See you in a mo.'

3.30pm

Benny rang.

He said, 'What is it with mothers?'

I said, 'What's the problem?'

He said, 'I've tidied my room, and what do I get?'

'Tell me.'

'I get, "Benjamin, do I really have to explain the word 'tidy' to you? Tidying means sorting out, clearing up and throwing away. It does not mean stuffing everything, including your dirty washing and that empty pizza box, under the bed."'

'Mmm,' I said. 'I suppose your mum does have a point.'

'No, she doesn't,' snapped Benny. 'I said to her, "Mum, there's tidying and then there's tidying.

And this is how we do it on <u>my</u> planet."'

'And she said?'

'She said, "Well, you're on <u>my</u> planet now, so go back to your room and don't come out until you've done it properly."'

● ● ● ● ● ● ● ● ● ● ● ● ● ● ● ● ● ● ●

Pause.

● ● ● ● ● ● ● ● ● ● ● ● ● ● ● ● ● ● ●

'So,' I said, 'looks like you won't be coming round today, then.'

'No,' he said. 'Looks like I won't.'

SUNDAY 6 AUGUST
After lunch
Really, REALLY full in the stomach department. Mum did rhubarb crumble for pudding because Benny and Paul are here.

Mum said, 'Would you like cream or ice cream or custard with that?'

Benny said, 'Can I have everything, please?'

Paul said, 'You've already had two helpings of roast potatoes and about four litres of gravy. You'll never eat "everything".'

'Bet I will,' answered Benny.

'Bet you won't,' replied Paul.

'Bet <u>you</u> couldn't,' returned Benny.

And that was it, really. The game was on. All three
of us had rhubarb crumble with cream <u>and</u> ice cream
<u>and</u> custard … and now none of us can move and Paul's
glasses have misted up.

'So, Dave,' said Benny, 'what are you writing?'

'Oh, you know,' I said, 'this and that.'

'Can <u>I</u> write something?' asked Paul.

'If you want,' I shrugged, and handed him my diary.

He wiped his glasses on his jeans and wrote:

**I have never been so full in the whole of my life.
Except possibly when we were on holiday and I
discovered honey-roast peanuts with raspberry
ripple ice cream.**

'**Eeew,**' Benny said.

'**Double eeew,**' I agreed. 'So, Benny, are you
looking forward to having Thomas to stay?'

'Kind of … sort of … don't really know,' said Benny.

'Who's Thomas?' Paul asked.

'The thing is,' said Benny, 'when little Jake came to
stay, I <u>so</u> didn't want him to, but actually it turned out
to be really cool.'

'Er – who's Thomas?' Paul asked.

'I was just being a bit selfish about it, I suppose – having to give up my room for Jake and Auntie Janice; not being able to do my own stuff all the time.'

'C'mon, guys, who's Thomas?' Paul asked.

'But then God showed me that Jake needed lots of love, so that's what I tried to give him.'

'Really pleased for you,' said Paul. 'But, who's Thomas?'

'So with Thomas coming,' Benny went on, 'I'm just trying to be … well … cool with it, I suppose. It's not like I have to move out of my room this time. We're putting up a camp bed for him next to my bookcase. Apparently he likes football, which is just wicked anyway, and he keeps fish.'

'Is he bringing the fish with him?' I asked.

'Wouldn't have thought so,' Benny answered. 'Can't be very easy travelling with a fish tank. But if he does, great, I suppose. I mean I've never shared my room with fish before.'

'You've never shared your room with someone from France before,' I said. 'How's he getting here?'

'He's doing the Channel Tunnel train thing with his dad. Then his dad's going right back and we're picking Thomas up from the station.'

'Great stuff,' I said.

Paul said, 'Um … this is all really interesting and everything and I could sit here listening to you two warbling on all day if I didn't have to go home soon, but for the last time –

WHO'S THOMAS?'

'Er, Paul,' I said, 'don't you know anything?'

6.30pm

I said, 'Benny, if Thomas is from France, how are you going to understand what he's saying?'

He said, 'No probs. He speaks English as well as French because his parents are English.'

'Wow,' I said. 'He's pretty clever then.'

'Clever enough,' Benny said. 'Mum just told me he does archery.'

'What's archery?'

'You know, using a bow and arrow.'

'What, sort of like Robin Hood?'

'Exactly like Robin Hood.'

'Why would anyone want to do that?' I asked.

'Why <u>wouldn't</u> anyone want to do that?' Benny answered. 'I can spend the whole summer being one of the Sherwood Forest gang – you know, a merry man.' He was beginning to sound quite excited.

I said, 'I think you'll find Robin Hood had more than one merry man.'

'I know that,' said Benny, 'but one's better than none.'

'I could be a merry man, too, if you like,' I offered.

'Yeah,' said Benny, 'it's just … well, you won't be around us the whole time so it's probably better if it's just me. Maybe you could be the evil Sheriff of Nottingham or something,

10

and we could be fighting against you to foil your dastardly plans.'

'Maybe,' I said. 'So, you're looking forward to Thomas coming now?'

'You bet.'

'Brill.'

6.45pm

Rang Benny.

I said, 'We'll still see each other a lot over the holidays, right?'

'Course,' he laughed. 'Thomas is going to love Topz. Anyway, got to go. I'm making a banner with Mum to put up when he gets here. It says "Welcome", only in French.'

'How do you know what "Welcome" is in French?' I asked.

'Mum told me. She knows quite a lot of French actually. She says she reckons that while Thomas is here, we ought to have times of the day when we only speak French with him. That'll help him feel at home and by the time we go back to school, I'll be able to speak in another language – well, a bit.

Is that stonking or is that stonking?'

'That's ... stonking,' I said.

11

7.00pm
Stonking but strangely weird.

In bed
Dad said, 'Everything all right?'
   I said, 'Everything's fine.'
   He asked, 'What have you got planned for the week?'
   I said, 'Don't really know.'
   He said, 'Something with Benny, no doubt.'
   I said, 'Maybe. Not sure. I think he's a bit busy.'
   Dad chuckled. 'Too busy for Dave the Rave?
I think not.'
   Oddly … I think so.

9.30pm
Lord God, it sounds as though things have been quite tough for Benny's sort-of-cousin-but-not lately with his mum being ill. Please help her to get better and give Thomas a really good holiday with Benny. And … well, please let there be a bit of time left over for Benny to spend with me, too. Amen.

MONDAY 7 AUGUST
12.30pm

Been shoe shopping with Mum. Well, I say shoe shopping. She got me to go to the shops with her by saying, 'Let's go and get you some new trainers,' and, to be fair, that's what I've got, new trainers.

But then she said, 'Let's just pop into Trents.'

I said, 'Mum, Trents is a knitting shop.'

She said, 'I know what it is, David.'

I said, 'Since when have you been interested in knitting?'

She said, 'Since I decided it was high time I learned a new skill.'

You see, that's the difference between Mum and me. If I was going to learn a new skill, knitting would be the last thing I'd think of.

I was just standing there thinking, 'Good job none of Topz can see me hanging around in a knitting shop,' when the door burst open.

'Dave! Never thought I'd see you in a knitting shop.' It was Sarah.

'Could be worse,' I thought.
'It could have been John.'

'So, Dave,' said John, following Sarah in through the shop doorway, 'how long have you been a secret knitter?'

'I am <u>not</u> a secret knitter,' I muttered. 'I am in here with my mum.'

'Of course you are,' nodded John. 'And she would be ...?'

'Over there,' I said, and pointed

13

her out where she stood inspecting some disgusting-looking, multi-coloured wool with purple bobbles.

'Knitting's nothing to be ashamed of, you know,' said John. 'I bet some of the world's most famous people are knitters.'

'And speaking of some of the world's most famous  people,' interrupted Sarah, 'well, people of the world anyway – did you know Benny's cousin, Thomas from France, does archery?'

'Thomas isn't his cousin,' I said. 'He's sort of like a cousin but that's a lot different to actually being a cousin. Saying Thomas is Benny's cousin is like saying dogs and cats are related.'

'They are actually,' said Sarah.

'No, they're not.'

'Yes, they are,' she insisted. 'Well, Saucy and Gruff are. They're both part of our family which means they've both got the same surname.'

'Anyway,' I said, knowing that with Sarah some things just aren't worth arguing about because you're never going to win, 'how do you know about Thomas liking archery?'

'Benny told me. And he told John. He's been telling everyone. He's dead excited about it. He's going to be a merry man or something.'

'Didn't know he'd been telling everyone,' I said. 'Didn't realise he was that fussed.'

'Oh, believe me, he is fussed,' replied Sarah. 'Incredibly fussed, isn't he, John?'

'Mega,' agreed John. 'Wouldn't stop going on about

it. Mind you,' he added, 'd'you know what I reckon he'd go on about even more if he knew?'

'No, what?'

'You being a secret knitter.'

Mum appeared holding up one of the disgusting balls of bobbly, multi-coloured wool.

'What do you think?' she asked. 'For your father?'

I hesitated. 'In ... what way?'

'Oh, I don't know, maybe for a sweater or something? Do you think he'd like the colours?'

'Um ...'

'I think he'd love them,' she decided. 'I'm going to get some of this.'

Groovy.

I looked at John and Sarah. They didn't say anything but I knew what they were thinking – 'Let's just hope that wool runs out before your mum starts on a sweater for you.'

2.00pm

Things don't usually niggle me. I'm not the niggly sort. I'm quite proud of that actually. Niggles happen and I just think, '<u>So</u> what? Get over it.'

I mean, I'm the one who always sorts out other people's niggles. That's because I'm generally niggleless and know better than to let silly little niggles get to me.

So what's going on?

Why am I feeling niggled?

2.05pm

Rang Benny.

I said, 'Do you want to come round? There's some left-over rhubarb crumble in the fridge with your name on it.'

He said, 'Sounds good, only I'm in the middle of something.'

'What's that?' I asked.

'Well,' he said, 'you know Thomas does archery? I'm making him a target.'

'A what?'

'A target. So he can practise his archery while he's here.'

'Benny,' I said, 'you can only do stuff like that where it's really safe. I'm sure your mum and dad won't let him practise archery in your flat. And anyway, you don't seriously think he's going to bring his bow and arrows with him, do you?'

'He might,' Benny said, 'but even if he doesn't, this is such a cool target. I'm using a bucket and a pillow. I mean, talk about genius. You have just got to see this.'

I would have asked how you make a target out of a bucket and a pillow, only, when he said the word 'genius', Benny managed to knock over the paint he was using to colour in the bull's eye and had to dash off to mop it up.

2.20pm

Benny rang.

'So,' he said, 'do you want to come round and take a look at this target, or what?'

'Definitely,' I said. 'Are we doing the Robin Hood thing?'

'Nah,' he said. 'But you know what you've got, don't you?'

'What?'

'Frog bean bags.'

In bed

I think Benny's right. I think he probably might be a genius. Well, a bit. Some of the time. I don't reckon he's a natural genius like Paul (but then, Paul's the one with the genius glasses). Still, with a bit of work, I'm sure he could get there. Let's face it, which other Topz would be able to come up with such an awesome idea for a target? Benny's painted a bull's eye on an old pillow, stuffed the bottom end of the pillow into a bucket, put the bucket on a stool and stood the whole thing against the hall wall next to the front door. His hall's fairly long and narrow, so that means you can stand quite far back to aim the bean bags. And there's nothing

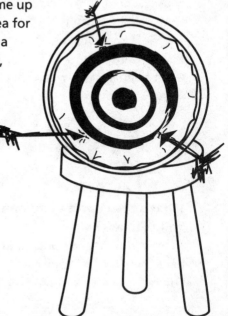

17

around to get broken if you happen to get one seriously off line, either. Although, having said that, his dad did come in through the front door unexpectedly. But, like he put it, 'It's not every day you get home from work to get smacked in the chest by a flying bean frog.'

Of course, when his dad mentioned beans, Benny realised he was hungry and we had to go and raid the freezer for choc-ices. We ate them in his room. That's when I sat in the wet patch on his bedroom carpet where he'd cleaned up the paint.

Bit later
Been down to get a drink. It's very hot tonight. Dad reckons we might have a storm. Mum was knitting.

Dad picked up the ball of bobbly wool and said, 'What's all this, then?'

Mum said, 'I'm knitting you a sweater.'

Dad said, 'I didn't know you could knit.'

Mum said, 'I can't.'

Still awake
Can't sleep. Hate it when that happens.

Grrrr...

(That's the sound of an annoyed person who's still still awake.)
After midnight now, and what am I doing? I'm lying here thinking, 'It's after midnight now and what am I doing?'

12.15am

Benny says they've got lots of things planned for when Thomas is here. They're going to do an open-top bus tour round London and see all the really cool places like Big Ben (or Big Benny as Benny calls it) and Tower Bridge, and then they're going to Madame Tussauds, the waxwork museum.

Benny said, 'I'm going to pretend to be a waxwork. I'm going to stand really still in a corner and when someone comes close to have a good look at me, I'm going to go, "**Boo!**".'

'The only thing is, all the waxworks are of famous people,' I said, 'and you're not exactly famous.'

He said, 'Yes, but I'm only pretending, aren't I? And if I'm only pretending, I can <u>pretend</u> to be a famous person who's <u>pretending</u> to be a waxwork. Who's going to know?'

But suddenly Benny was being all serious. 'Do you think Thomas will be all right?' he frowned. 'I mean, he's going to be a long way from home and his mum's not well. Supposing he gets really down and homesick and I don't know the right thing to say? Supposing he thinks my target's just really stupid? Supposing he thinks I'<u>m</u> just really stupid?'

And that's when I realised. Benny was actually worried about Thomas being here. He doesn't usually

19

get bothered by things like that. How could I have missed it? I just thought he was Benny-style excited.

I said, 'Thomas'll be fine. He can't think you're stupid because actually you're almost a genius. I mean, that's nearly as much of a genius as Paul. And anyway, you won't be on your own. We'll all be here to help him have a good time. How about I ask Mum if we can have a Topz barbecue at our house one day this week so he can meet us all? You know what my dad's like about barbecues – any excuse. What do you reckon?'

'I reckon … cool. Thanks.'

12.25am

Thank You, Lord, that You've given me Benny as my best friend. After all, everyone should have an almost genius in their life.

Everyone should have <u>You</u> in their life, too. Benny says Thomas is one of Your friends, so I guess he's been talking to You about coming to England anyway, but please be with him, Lord. Help him to know that You're close to him and that, even though he's going to be away from home in a different country, he's not on his own. You <u>never</u> leave us on our own. Brilliant. Amen.

12.30am

Uh oh … was that thunder?

12.32am

Yup. Dad was right. There's going to be a storm …

TUESDAY 8 AUGUST

7.30am

I reckon that's one of the worst sleeps I've ever had. In fact it wasn't a sleep at all, it was an awake. A wide awake. Most of the night. If the thunder and lightning weren't crashing and flashing around, the rain was hurling itself about as if someone was throwing drawing pins up against my window. A lot of drawing pins.

The lightning was pretty incredible, though. I sat watching for a while. There was just rain pouring down and then all of a sudden a huge, straggly streak of lightning would shoot across the sky – like a massive, flaring crack appearing.

Awesome.

Truly.

7.45am

Mum says nothing's working because the electricity's gone off. Dad thinks something might have got hit during the thunderstorm. Mum says he's not happy – he had to go to work without having his usual bowl of porridge. Although, how he can eat porridge when the weather's this hot and sticky, I'll never know. Mum says he's a creature of habit. I think he's just weird.

Anyway, Mum says she's going to give it another half an hour and if the power's not back on by then, we've got a small camping stove in the garage so she'll be able to boil the kettle for a cup of tea.

'Porridge Dad can do without,' she said. 'Tea I can't.'

7.50am

Danny rang. At least the phone's still working.

'Have you heard?' he asked.

'About what?' I said.

'The community centre.'

'What about it?'

'A tree fell through it.'

'A what?'

'A tree.'

'You're kidding,' I said. 'How?'

'Got struck by lightning in the night,' he replied. 'That was a really bad storm.'

7.55am

Put the phone down and it rang again straight away.

'Have you heard about the community centre?' It was Paul.

'I know,' I said. 'Danny just rang. Bad, isn't it?'

'I'm going down with Dad soon to have a look. Do you want to come?'

'Wow, yeah!'

'See you in a bit, then.'

8.00am

Rang Benny.

I said, 'Sounds like that thunderstorm's done some real damage.'

He said, 'What thunderstorm? When?'

I said, 'The one in the night. Didn't you hear it?'

He said, 'Well, I wouldn't have, would I? I was asleep.'

8.05am

Asked Benny if he wanted to come down with Paul and me to the community centre to see what's happened, but he can't because of going to pick up Thomas. They haven't got any electricity either. I told him if it wasn't back on by tonight, they could all come round here and we could do the barbecue. Dad'll be fine with it, I'm sure. After all, we've got to eat.

8.10am

I wonder if you can barbecue porridge?

9.30am

Electricity back now. Just as well. Mum was complaining about her mouth shrivelling up like a weed on a compost heap due to lack of tea. As it turned out, she couldn't find the camping stove.

12.30pm

Kind of a mess down at the community centre, although Greg pointed out that it could have been a lot worse. He said how great that it happened at night, for instance, so no one was around to get hurt.

Greg is so definitely cool. I mean, he's really busy being our church youth leader but if anything happens around Holly Hill, he's right there lending a hand. He does exactly what he tells us we should try to do. He always says being a Christian isn't about shutting yourself off from the world and only doing church things with church people. It's about getting out there and helping where you can wherever you are. You know, making a difference. Showing people that Jesus is your best friend and how much He means to you by being kind and loving to others; supporting people when they need it; sharing their upsets and being happy with them when good things happen.

So anyway, there was Greg this morning doing just that. Mr Carter, the centre caretaker, was tut-tutting and shaking his head and saying things like, 'It's going to take more than a good sweeping to get this lot cleared up', and, 'My back won't stand for it, it's already aching like a good 'un', and Mrs Peach who does all the bookings was practically in tears. She said they're supposed to have a group in later today for a wildlife talk, and where, oh where, was Tuesday night bingo going to be held? Greg said he was sure it wouldn't be a problem to transfer the community centre events to the church hall until the mess was sorted out.

Personally, I think it's a lot of fuss about nothing. OK, so a tree's fallen down but it didn't land on the building like everyone thought. It wasn't tall enough to reach. What it's actually done is squash a couple of wooden sheds round the back and broken three windows – and, let's face it, Mr Carter, it's not going to take long to sweep up the glass from those. The biggest job Greg said is to get the tree chopped up and taken away, and he's offered to arrange all that this afternoon. Paul and I, we said we could help, but Greg said what would be really useful was if we could lend a hand with all the repainting where everything's got a bit scuffed up. Cool.

12.45pm
Wonder if Thomas is in England yet?

24

5.30pm

Went round to the park. Paul said he'd meet me down there after lunch for – wait for it – leapfrog. Danny turned up with a ball wanting to play a spot of footie, but Paul said was there any way we could combine that with the leapfrog thing.

Danny said, 'Sure. You've ~~been~~ doing leapfrog. Now let's play football.'

Paul said, 'But that's not exactly a combination, is it?'

Danny answered, 'Well, football's not exactly the kind of thing you can combine with leapfrog. How many football matches have you been to where a player kicks the ball then leapfrogs over the guy next to him to take a shot at goal?'

'Do you know what, that's a brilliant idea,' said Paul. 'Knew you'd come up with something.'

So that's what we did. We took turns being in goal and whoever's turn it was at kicking had to kick the ball, then leapfrog over whoever wasn't in goal before trying to get the ball in the net.

'I reckon this could really catch on,' said Paul. 'We could call it "frogball" … or "leapfoot". What do think?'

I was very hot. I said, 'I think it's time to go back to my house and raid the fridge.'

7.00pm

All set for the barbecue for Thomas tomorrow evening. Paul and Danny can both come. I've spoken to the other Topzies, except Josie who's out, and they can all make it too – and Sarah said if Josie had anything planned for tomorrow she'd know about it because she knows everything there is to know about Josie and probably more than that. Pretty sure the whole Gang'll be there.

7.10pm
Groovy. Rang Benny. All systems **go go GO** for tomorrow. Weird phone call, though. But I guess a lot of my phone calls with Benny are weird. That said, at least they're usually in English which, from my point of view (being English), makes things a whole lot easier. This one wasn't entirely – in English, that is … I don't think.

It went something like –

Me: Hey, Benny. Did you pick up Thomas all right?
Benny: *May wee.*
Me: Sorry?
Benny: It's French.
Me: Oh. Cool. And in English that would be …?
Benny: Er … yes.
Me: Yes, what?
Benny: No, that's what *'may wee'* is in English. Yes. At least I think that's what Thomas said.
Me: Oh, great, so you did pick him up all right?
Benny: *May wee.*

Pause.

Me: So anyway, Topz welcome barbecue for Thomas all arranged for tomorrow evening at my house. You'll both be there, won't you?
Benny: *May wee* … um … *Tray bonne.*
Me: I suppose that would mean 'yes'?

Benny: Yes and double stonking.

Me: Cool. See you there.

Benny: *May wee.* Would you like to *parlay* to Thomas?

Me: Would I like to what?

Benny: You know, *parlay*. Talk.

Me: Will I be able to understand what he's saying?

Benny: *May wee.* His *Onglay* is really *tray bonne*.

Me: I've no idea what you're talking about, but I'll give it a go. Can't be any more confusing than having a conversation with you.

Benny: What d'you mean? I reckon I *parlay Fronsay* really well, and I've only been learning for a couple hours.

Me: Yes, I think the problem could be that I don't *parlay Frons* … wotsit at all and that's what's making it slightly tricky.

Pause.

Benny: *May wee* … I mean, oh yeah, I never thought of that. I'll get Thomas.

Me: No, that's OK. I'll speak to him tomorrow.

Benny: When?

Me: At the barbecue.

Benny: Oh, yeah.

Me: You will both be there won't you, Benny?

Benny: *May wee.*

Me: See you then.

Benny: *May wee and tray bo–*

That's when I put the phone down. Sometimes with Benny, it's the best way.

WEDNESDAY 9 AUGUST — BARBECUE DAY!

After breakfast

Loads to do. I've got to plan what we're going to
barbecue, organise what games we're going to play,
make a list of everything we've got to buy, and go with
Mum to get the shopping.

Mum said, 'Have you got salad on your list?'

I said, 'Not especially, no. This is a barbecue.'

Mum said, 'Yes, but you have to have salad.
Just because it's a barbecue doesn't make it a
vegetable-free zone.'

I said, 'It's not going to be a vegetable-free zone.
There'll be fried onions with the burgers, and
tomato ketchup.'

10.30am

Rang Paul.

I said, 'I thought we could
have a games marathon
tonight. Have you still got
your box of Scrabble? Only,
if you have, would you mind bringing it over so we
could maybe have a game later?'

Paul said, 'I thought you'd got Scrabble?'

I said, 'We have, but all the Bs, Ps and Ns are missing.'

'How come?' he asked.

'Because,' I said, 'when Mum was planting some seeds
last year, she used them as little markers so she'd know
which plants she'd put in which pots.'

'How did that work, then?'

'Haven't a clue but she was really pleased with her hanging baskets. So, like I say, please can we borrow yours?'

'Yupdeedoody,' said Paul. 'I can bring Snakes and Ladders, too. And Cluedo.'

'Triffic. Thanks a lot.'

'No probs. You're a lot welcome.'

10.40am

Josie rang.

She said, 'Dad's made chocolate ice cream with chocolate chunks. Shall I bring some to the barbecue?'

I said, 'Wow! Do you really need to ask?'

She said, 'Not if it was just Topz, obviously, but do you think Thomas will like it? I don't know if they eat ice cream in France.'

'Who cares?' I said. 'I like it. Bring it on!'

10.50am

Rang Danny.

I said, 'Can you bring round a couple of footballs later? I've only got one here. Thought we could have a keepy-uppy contest.'

He said, 'Does Thomas play football?'

'Dunno,' I said, 'but Benny'll love it.'

10.55am

Rang Benny to ask him to bring his target over this evening for frog bag-throwing.

No answer.

1.00pm

Just got back with the shopping. Tons of it. What is it with parents and vegetables? I'm sure we've got more cabbages than there are rabbits in the world to eat them, and don't even get me started on the number of carrots.

Mum said, 'I'm going to make you all some delicious coleslaw.'

I said, 'Mum, it's really kind of you and everything but, honestly, all anyone's really going to be interested in is burgers.'

She said, 'And where are the vitamins in those, I'd like to know? Now, I'm making coleslaw and you're all going to have at least a spoonful. Otherwise, David,' she added, 'I may have to start knitting you a sweater ...'

2.30pm

Everything going to plan.

Brilliant.

Stonking.

Cool as a cucumber in a fish tank with no fish but lots of ice cubes.

2.35pm

Still no reply at Benny's.

4.00pm

Mum's put sunflower seeds in the coleslaw.

I said, 'Mum, we're not hamsters.'

Mum said, 'Yes, but have you seen what incredibly long, strong teeth hamsters have? And have you noticed how bright their eyes are? And do you realise what outstanding brains they've got? I mean, no one teaches them to run round and round in one of those wheel things they have in their cages. They just work it out all by themselves.'

'All of which would mean ...?'

'All of which would mean, David,' Mum finished, 'that sunflower seeds are obviously a powerhouse among foods, and they are not to be tossed aside lightly.'

Just tossed into coleslaw, obviously.

4.30pm
Rang Benny. Again. Still no answer. They must be out for the day. Weird. He didn't say they were going out for the day. Guess they'll be back any minute.

4.32pm
Tried again. No one there. Maybe not 'any minute' then, but soon.

4.45pm
Phone rang.

I yelled down to Mum, 'I'll get it. It's bound to be Benny.'

It wasn't. It was Greg.

He said, 'Are you free to do some painting at the community centre tomorrow morning?'

I said, 'I think so.'

He said, 'Great. See if you can round up some troops

and we can meet there at about half past ten.'

'No probs,' I said. 'Having a Topzy barbecue in a bit to welcome Benny's sort-of-cousin-but-not, Thomas. I'll find out who's free.'

5.30pm
Don't know where Benny's got to, but he's really annoying. How can I get him to bring his target over this evening if no one's there to answer the phone?

5.40pm
Sometimes it really stinks being Benny's best friend.

11.30pm
Did I say stinks? Not bad enough. Not NEARLY bad enough. How about, being Benny's best friend is the worst, most horrible, most disgusting, most

MEGA RATTY THING IN THE WHOLE, ENTIRE, MASSIVE WORLD, PLANET, UNIVERSE, GALAXY, INFINITY OF INFINITIES?

11.35pm
Yeah. That's much better.

THURSDAY 10 AUGUST
8.00am
Great welcome barbecue for Thomas.

Wicked.

Awesome.

There were just a couple of things missing, though. Let me see, what were they?

Oh, yeah.

Benny and Thomas.

4.00pm
Met Greg down at the community centre this morning for painting over tree damage with Paul, Josie and Danny.

Greg said, 'Is it just me, Dave, or has something seriously rattled your chain since I spoke to you yesterday?'

'Whatever gives you that idea?' I grunted.

'Oh, I don't know,' he said. 'It could be the way you've been grinding your teeth since you got here, you've barely said two words to anybody, and you look as though you're trying to squeeze the life out of that paintbrush. What's up?'

I looked at Paul. He shrugged.

'You may as well say,' sighed Josie. 'He's bound to find out anyway.'

So I told him. I told him how I'd spent hours organising a welcome barbecue for Benny's sort-of-cousin-but-not, Thomas. I explained how the plan was for burgers and sunflower seed coleslaw. I went through all the games we'd got together for the games marathon. I described how the chocolate chunks in Josie's dad's ice cream were the size of great big

33

boulders and looked absolutely awesome. I said how everything was ready way before everyone was due to arrive, so I got in some keepy-uppy practice and actually managed 41, which has got to be my best score ever.

And then I told Greg how it was all <u>a complete and utter waste of time and effort</u> because Benny and Thomas never showed up. Benny and Thomas had gone out for the day with Benny's parents to the marine aquarium. They'd had a wicked time – really stonking Benny told me when I rang him for the last time at half past nine yesterday evening. On the way back, his dad

had suggested stopping for a fish and chip supper to give Thomas a taste of something well and truly English after his first full day here. Benny thought that was a great idea and was so excited about being the one to introduce Thomas to batter and salt 'n' vinegar and mushy peas that he forgot all about the barbecue. They all did.

Benny said he was sorry, really, really sorry, but at least I'd had a good time with all the other Topz.

I **shouted** at him and told him he was a **complete and utter dimwit** and having a good time with the other Topz wasn't the point. The point of the barbecue was to welcome Thomas.

'Was it?' Benny said. 'Oops, sorry. Must have missed that bit somewhere.'

'Too right you missed it,' I growled. 'There's something else you've missed, too. I'm supposed to be your best friend. Your best friend in the whole world. Funny that. All it takes is Thomas, the sort-of-cousin-but-not, to turn up and all of a sudden you've thrown me out with the ... **pig food**.'

Silence. Then –

'I don't have any pig food,' Benny said.

'**No?**' I snapped. '**Well, if you did, you'd have just thrown it all over me!**'

And that was it, really. End of the story of the waste-of-time barbecue. End of the summer holiday good times.

End of a best friendship.

In bed

Greg came round after supper.

He said, 'Don't let something like this mess up your friendship with Benny. I agree it was all a bit thoughtless of him, but he didn't let you down deliberately. You know what he's like when he gets over-excited about something – the moon could turn green and he wouldn't notice. I had a chat with him earlier and, under all that hair, you know, he really is very sorry.'

I just shrugged. 'I don't care how sorry he is. Besides, Benny's not my friend. If he was, Thomas wouldn't have been able to get between us like that. I mean, he's hardly been here two days and Benny's lost interest in me already.'

'Thomas hasn't got between you. Whatever gives you that idea?' Greg said. 'And Benny hasn't lost interest. He's just got a lot of other things on his mind – like how to help Thomas feel welcome.'

'But that's exactly what I was trying to do,' I said, 'give Thomas a Topz welcome to Holly Hill. So much for that, though. Anyway, I don't care about him any more. And I don't care about Benny either. He doesn't deserve me as a friend. Neither of them do.'

10.30pm

Lord God, of all the people I could have been best friends with, why did you have to make it Benny? He's such an airhead. I've had it up to here with him. He's always coming up with stupid ideas. And now he's made me look like a total idiot for doing something really special for him when all he's interested in is his pointless sort-of-cousin-but-not.

Greg says he understands what's in my head, but he doesn't. He says it's easy to feel that people don't deserve friendship or love when they've let us down, but we have to try and forgive them, just like You do – after all, we let You down all the time with the wrong things we do, but You still want to be our friend. Greg says You give us love we don't deserve every day, which is what we should do for each other.

I guess You love Benny right now, Lord, but I don't think I like him very much any more. And one thing's for sure. I understand why I've had this niggle for the last few days. I just knew Thomas was going to come between Benny and me, and he has. Always trust your niggles, that's what I say.

Well, Benny's lost me as a friend and that's all there is to it. The worst thing is, now he's got Thomas, I don't suppose he'll even notice. The other worst thing is, You don't want us to get angry with each other and end up quarrelling, and usually it's the last thing I do. So Benny's really hurt me and he's made me do something that makes You unhappy. I'm sorry for that, but it's not my fault. I can't help how I feel. I just can't.

FRIDAY 11 AUGUST

After breakfast

Benny rang.

He said, 'What are you up to?'

I said, 'Nothing.'

He said, 'Well, what would you like to be up to?'

I said, 'Nothing.'

He said, 'Would you like to come round here?'

I said, 'Nope.'

He said, 'Oh, go on. Thomas and me,

we thought if you wanted to come round with your frog bags, we could all do some target practice.'

I said, 'I don't do target practice any more.'

He said, 'Why not?'

I said, 'If you have to ask, you're even more of a dimwit than I already thought you were.'

Benny said, 'If this is about the barbecue, I've said I'm really sorry. I know I should have listened better when you rang and invited us. I was excited and I just wasn't really concentrating. But, hey, it's not every day you get someone who speaks French coming to stay.'

'No,' I said. 'It's not every day you let your best friend down **stonkingly spectacularly** either, is it, Benny?'

9.30pm – In bed

Benny didn't ring again today.

Good.

9.35pm

Dear Lord God, I'm sorry but I just can't do it. I can't be a friend to someone who doesn't deserve it. You can carry on loving Benny if You want to, but I'm done.

9.40pm

Done with a capital **'D'**.

SUNDAY 13 AUGUST

2.30pm

Sunday Club was painful for two reasons:

1. I fell over a chair whilst trying to avoid coming face to face with the sort-of-cousin-but-not.

2. I didn't manage to avoid coming face to face with the sort-of-cousin-but-not.

2.35pm

Sometimes falling over things is SO worth it if you end up with a totally amazing-looking bruise. When I first fell over the chair, this unbelievably wicked-looking lump came up on my shin and I was looking forward to a **STONKER** of a bluey-greeny great bruise that I'd be able to show off for days. But now, there's practically nothing there – no more lump even, just a bit of a red mark. Rubbish, actually.

3.00pm

Greg said, 'Thomas seems like a nice lad, doesn't he?'

I said, 'I wouldn't know. All we did was sort of look at each other. He did say, "Are you all right?" as I was picking myself up off the floor, but that's about it.'

Greg said, 'You should have a chat with him. I think you two'll get on like a house on fire. I bet you didn't know, for instance, that Thomas is really into cycling, like you.'

'Oh,' I said. 'I thought he was "really into" archery.'

'That, too,' Greg replied, 'but that's not something _you_ do. Whereas bikes – you and Thomas have got that in common.'

I said, 'We've got noses in common, but that doesn't make him my new best mate.'

Greg said, 'I know you're still angry, Dave, but just be careful. Don't let your angry thoughts lead you into doing … well … angry things.'

Whatever that's supposed to mean.

3.45pm **just don't**

You see, like I said to Josie while she was helping me pick the chair up, there are days when you feel like meeting new people and chatting till your tongue drops off, and days when you just don't. And today was one of those 'just don't' days.

just don't

4.00pm

Anyway, like Josie said to me, whoever heard of Robin Hood on a bicycle?

In bed

Mum came in and said, 'So? What do you think?'

She was holding up what looked like a cross between a sack and something I might have drawn when I was two years old.

'Umm …' I knew I had to be careful here. 'I'm not sure. Is that …?'

'It's Dad's sweater, what did you think it was? I've just finished knitting it, and I don't think I've done a bad job, if I do say so myself. Obviously there's the odd mistake in there, but I don't think your dad will notice, do you? And even if he does, what does he expect from something homemade? If you want a sweater to be perfect, go and buy one from the shops, that's what I say.'

Fortunately, Mum was in one of those moods for not letting anyone get a word in edgeways, so I got away with just smiling and nodding in an agreeing-with-everything-she-was-saying kind of way. Which is just as well because, as homemade sweaters go, this one was awesomely awful – and I'm not being unkind, I'm just being … well … honest.

'When are you going to give it to him, then?' I asked, when there was a long enough gap to say something.

'Not sure. I was thinking of maybe hanging on to it and bringing it out as a surprise for Christmas.'

'But how can it be a surprise? Dad knows you're knitting it.'

'Oh, he'll have forgotten by then,' she said cheerfully. 'I once bought him a pair of slippers for his birthday which he put in the bottom of the wardrobe and forgot all about. So on his next birthday, I got them out, wrapped them up, and gave them to him all over again. He never remembered a thing.'

Pause.

'Besides,' she added, 'your dad's got a lot more on his mind at the moment than my knitting.'

'Like what?'

'Oh, you know your dad,' she finished, a bit hurriedly I thought. 'Always thinking about something. Night night, Davey.'

'Night, Mum.'

Odd.

MONDAY 14 AUGUST

10.00am

Paul rang.

He said, 'Greg just phoned. Carnival planning meeting's definitely on for this evening. See you there?'

'Yup, see you there,' I said.

10.05am

Greg rang.

He said, 'Just to let you know the carnival planning meeting's definitely on for this evening.'

I said, 'I know.'

He said, 'Oh.'

I said, 'Paul rang.'

He said, 'Ah.'

I said, 'See you there.'

He said, 'Uh huh.'

Sometimes talking to Greg makes me realise how unimportant words really are.

4.30pm

We've got it! Me, Josie and Sarah! Sunday Club is going to have the best float in the whole of the Holly Hill carnival. This is the wickedest idea! I mean, everyone is going to be blown away by it. Totally.

Boom-bang-boom!

We were down at the park after lunch. Things were feeling a bit on the flat side because Josie had made a really big thing to Sarah about my bruise from yesterday, and then when they both saw it (or rather saw the tiny red mark where the bruise should have been) they were a bit, 'Is that it? I've seen more damage on a banana.'

But then Josie suddenly said, 'Why don't we try and come up with a completely and utterly brilliantly brilliant theme for the float? Then we don't have to waste time at the meeting this evening talking about what it's actually going to be – which, let's face it, could take hours like last year, especially if Benny's there going on about doing an alien pizza café or a hot dog bus stop again. Instead, we can spend the time deciding who's going to organise what and talking about costumes.'

So that's what we did. We went back to Josie's and decided what theme we wanted to do. Then we got some paper and drew sort of how the float could look – at least Josie and Sarah did because I'm about as good with a pencil as Mum seems to be with knitting needles – and zam, bap, quicker-than-that, our Sunday Club carnival float idea was well and truly … floating!

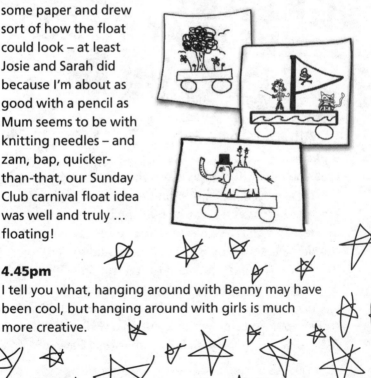

4.45pm

I tell you what, hanging around with Benny may have been cool, but hanging around with girls is much more creative.

5.00pm

This meeting's going to be great. It's about the Sunday Club float, which has everything to do with Sunday Club and Topz and the Holly Hill carnival, and nothing whatsoever to do with anyone's sort-of-cousin-but-not. That means that even if Benny shows up, Thomas won't because, why would he when it's got nothing to do with him? After all, he's never going to be in Topz, let alone the carnival.

In bed

If I was all on my own at the very, very top of a lonely mountain in the middle of nowhere right now, I'd

SCREAM
THE PLACE
DOWN...

TUESDAY 15 AUGUST
6.00am

I tell you what, if Thomas keeps showing up where he's not wanted, he's not going to make any friends. I mean, there was no way he had any business being at Greg's for that carnival meeting yesterday. Benny should have told him. He should have said to him, 'No, sorry, Thomas, you need to stay at home. This meeting's nothing to do with you. You're not invited.'

Only Benny didn't, did he? He obviously said, 'Of course you can come with me, Thomas. Everyone'll be really pleased to see you. Everyone except Dave, of course, but then you already know he doesn't count.'

I'm fed up with it. This has got to be the worst summer of my life. Josie, Sarah and me, we had the best idea for that carnival float: a pirate ship. That's better than anything. But just because, according to Greg, Thomas is 'a new friend who's only with us for a short time', for some reason, he got to choose the theme. And everyone seemed to be OK with that – even Josie and Sarah. I mean, what is it with Topz at the moment?

And I'll tell you something else for nothing: there is no way I'm standing on that float under a fake tree being a merry man for Thomas's stupid Robin Hood idea. Not in a million years. Not in a million, trillion, billion, **ZILLION** even. Never.

9.00am

Benny rang.

I said, 'What?'

He said, 'Just wanted to say I thought the pirate idea was really good, too.'

I said, 'You still voted for Robin Hood, though.'

He said, 'Yeah, well, it's difficult. Thomas isn't here for very long and –'

'Exactly!' I snapped. 'He's not here for very long. That's because, in case you hadn't noticed, he doesn't live here. He's got nothing to do with Topz and I wish he'd just GO HOME.'

Then Benny said it. Not angrily or shoutily. Not even unkindly.

He just said, 'You know what I think, don't you? I think you're jealous of Thomas. I think you've been jealous of him ever since you heard he was coming to stay with me. And it's so stupid because he's just someone having a bit of a hard time who's here for a few weeks. Forgetting about the barbecue was <u>my</u> fault, not his. He's not trying to push you out or shove his way in. If he'd come to stay with anyone else, I don't think you'd mind. It's because he's hanging out with <u>me</u> all the time. I know the holidays are a bit

different now from how we thought they were going to be but, believe it or not, Dave, you're still my best mate.'

9.15am

I don't know what he's going on about. I've never been jealous of anyone in my life.

9.20am

I mean, why's he talking like that? And why would I be jealous of Thomas anyway? I don't even know him. I don't <u>want</u> to know him. No, this is all Benny's fault. He's the one who's the big let down – the one who's more interested in doing things with a sort-of-cousin-but-not rather than with me. How does that make me jealous?

9.30am

He's got it all wrong. Benny <u>always</u> gets everything all wrong. I wouldn't even know **HOW** to be jealous.

2.30pm

Paul and John came round. They were wearing shorts. I must have looked confused because John said, 'Duh!'

'Duh … what?' I shrugged.

'The fun run?' said Paul. 'On Friday evening? The one Benny didn't want to do so you asked us to do it with you? You haven't forgotten already?'

'I had actually.'

'Well, you'd better start remembering,' John went on, 'because if we don't get in some seriously funny running before then, we're going to be left standing like a row of skittles that have been left … standing.'

We were on our third lap round the park when Paul huffed, 'I think giving the money we raise at the carnival to the community centre is a brill-baggins idea, don't you?'

'Who said anything about giving it to the community centre?' I asked.

'Greg did. Last night? Don't tell me you've forgotten that as well?'

'No,' I puffed. 'I just don't remember him mentioning the community centre, that's all.'

John said, 'I'm not surprised. You were too busy looking daggers at Thomas.'

'What?'

If I could have screeched to a halt at that moment, I would have done. As it was, I stopped silently dead and Paul ran smack into me.

'WHAT?' I said again.

'Well, I know you don't like Thomas,' John went on, 'but you could try and make it a tiny bit less obvious.'

'I don't not like Thomas at all,' I said. 'I've hardly said two words to him. In fact I don't even think I've said that many. How can I not like someone I've said no words to?'

JEALOUS JEALOUS JEALOUS JEALOUS JEALOU JEALOUS ALOUS JEALOUS JEALOUS JEALOUS JEALOUS JEALOUS JEALOU JEALOUS JEALOUS

EALOUS 'Exactly,' said John. 'He's been here for days and you haven't even talked to him. Benny says it's because you're <u>jealous.</u>'

Just the sound of that word sent prickles crawling up my back.

'Huh?'

'He wasn't being mean or anything,' added Paul quickly. 'He just thinks it's a bit of shame because you've got nothing to be jealous about.'

I stared at them. 'Is that what you think, too?' I asked. 'That I'm jealous of Thomas because he's come to stay with Benny?'

'Not really,' said Paul. 'But you didn't look happy when Robin Hood got chosen over pirates.'

'Because Robin Hood is a really rubbish idea and pirates is a really good one!' I argued.

rubbish rubbish rubbish rubbish rubbish rubbish rubbish rubbish rubbish rubbish rubbish rubbish rubbish rubbish rubbish rubbish rubbish rubbish rubbish

'Well,' John began slowly, 'we all thought Robin Hood was quite good, too. I mean, I quite fancy being a merry man and Sarah's dead excited because she's going to be Maid Marion.'

'And anyway,' said Paul, 'does it really matter that much as long as we raise some money? Greg said it would be brilliant if Sunday Club could pay for some new bushes and flowers to be planted behind the community centre where the tree fell down.'

'Yeah?' I said. 'Well, Sunday Club can get on and pay for it without me. I don't want to be Robin Hood, a merry man, the Sheriff of Nottingham <u>or</u> Maid Marion. You're all just totally … sad.'

I started to walk away.

'Oh, come on, Dave,' called Paul. 'At least let's finish funny running.'

I didn't even look round, just snarled over my

SNARL SNARL SNARL SNARL SNARL SNARL SNARL SNARL SNARL SNARL SNARL SNARL SNARL SNARL SNARL SNARL shoulder, 'There's nothing funny about any of this. And the only place I'm running is home.'

4.30pm

Lying on my bed, staring at the ceiling. It's all white except for two black dots right over where my feet are. I thought they might be flies but they can't be or they'd have moved by now. In which case, I've no idea what they are or how they got there. I've never even noticed them before. But then I've never spent so long lying on my bed staring up at the ceiling before. I'm trying to hear God. Greg says talking to God is brilliant but so is listening to Him, and you can't listen to Him if you don't stop and spend a bit of time being quiet.

To be honest, it's not totally quiet. Mr Holly next door is mowing his lawn and he's got a really loud lawn mower. I shut the window for a while but then it was just boiling in here, so I had to open it again.

I've often wondered whether Mr Holly moved to Holly Hill because his name is Mr Holly or whether he's just someone called Mr Holly who just happens to live in Holly Hill. Paul says I should ask him, but I think that might be a bit rude. I mean, my surname's Howell, and if this was Howell Hill instead of Holly Hill, I wouldn't particularly want people coming up to me and saying, 'Did you move here because you're a Howell and this is Howell Hill or did it just happen?'

And that's the other part of the problem I'm having hearing God. I can't stop thinking. For all I know, He's out there trying desperately to get a word in, but can't because there's so much other stuff going on in my head.

You see, I'm not jealous of Thomas. I'm just not. What I'm waiting for God to tell me is that He understands and … that He's on my side.

6.00pm

Mum says I've got the most miserable-looking face she's seen since Dad got sunburnt painting the garden fence because he 'didn't think it was that hot'.

I said, 'Thanks.'

She said, 'You're welcome. Now, either cheer up or tell me what the problem is. You're not still fretting about Benny and the barbecue? He wouldn't have let you down on purpose, you know, he's your best friend.'

'Was my best friend,' I answered. 'Now all he cares about is Thomas.'

'Oh, you know that's not true!' Mum laughed. 'Thomas is just staying with Benny for a while. You could join in with everything they're doing except you don't seem to want to.'

'And why would I want to? Thomas isn't my sort-of-cousin-but-not.'

Then Mum said it. Just like everyone else is saying it. 'Do I detect a hint of jealousy?'

'No!' I shouted it out. I knew I shouldn't shout but I just did. 'Why does everyone think that?'

'Everyone?'

'Yes, everyone! Benny, Paul, John. Now even you.'

'Maybe it's because behaving the way you are at the moment is just not like you,' she said quietly, which made my shouting seem even louder. 'You're usually so kind and welcoming to everyone. You're usually the peacemaker. That's probably all Thomas wants. A bit of peace. He's not had a very happy time lately with his mum being in hospital. This is a chance for him to enjoy a little break. I'm sure the last thing he's after is spoiling things between you and Benny.'

'Is that why God's not talking to me?' I grunted. 'Because <u>He</u> thinks I'm jealous, too?'

'Maybe God <u>is</u> talking to you,' Mum said, putting her arm round my shoulder and giving it a squeeze. 'Maybe He's speaking to you through the people who love you. God can see you're not happy, and if you <u>are</u> a bit jealous then that's probably why. He doesn't want your summer spoilt by bad feelings, so perhaps He's been using other people to point them out to you. I bet He's saying right now, "I can see what's going on here, Davey. Those jealous thoughts? Just say you're sorry and leave them with me. I'll deal with them."'

Then Mum added something that really surprised me.

She said, 'I had a problem with jealousy

once, you know. A few years before you were born, when I was still a nurse, my best friend and I ended up applying for the same job in the same hospital. I really wanted that job, and I prayed like mad that I'd get it, but in the end my friend was chosen instead of me. I was so cross. I didn't speak to God for days because I thought it was all His fault. I didn't speak to my friend for quite a while, either.

'What I should have done was pray. I could have said, "Thank You, Lord, for my friend and for making sure that new job at the hospital is in really safe hands with her. Help me not to be disappointed. I know You'll put me in the right job at the right time because You want what's best for me." But instead of trusting God to take care of my future, I made myself really miserable by being jealous of someone who was actually far better in that particular job than I would ever have been. Don't waste your time having bad thoughts, Davey. You need to get rid of them; hand them over to God. He'll deal with them because He's the one who truly understands us. When you do that, that's when you'll get your peace back – and get rid of that grumpy old face. Believe me, I know what I'm talking about.'

8.00pm
It's weird how SO many different people who say they care about me can get me SO wrong. I'm not jealous. Why am I the only one who seems to realise that? Mum and her job – that was a totally different situation. She wanted something her friend had. Thomas, on the other hand, hasn't got anything I could <u>possibly</u> want. I mean, it's not like I'm desperate to do archery but haven't got a bow and arrow.

So thanks for the advice, everyone, but no thanks. If I'm not happy it's because Benny's let me down, not because I'm having 'bad thoughts'. Besides, if God's the one who truly understands me, then He'll know that the <u>last</u> thing I am is jealous of Thomas.

And you know what? I'm going to prove it.

WEDNESDAY 16 AUGUST

THE PLAN

Step 1:
Arrange another barbecue and invite Benny and Thomas.

Step 2:
Ask Thomas if he'd like to join in fun run on Friday.

Step 3:
Lend Thomas my bike so he can go cycling with Benny (although possibly that is going a bit far).

Step 4:
Tell Thomas that Robin Hood is cooler than pirates for carnival float.

Step 5:
Invite Thomas to stay next time he comes to England for holiday.

Perfecto-confecto or what! If I do all that for Thomas, no one, and I mean NO ONE, can stand up and say, 'Eeew, look at Dave – he's all jealous!' Someone who's jealous would not invite the person they're supposed to be jealous of to do <u>anything</u>, let alone come round to their house for a barbecue, and the last thing they'd do is lend them their bike. They're all going to have to face up to it: **THEY'RE WRONG.**

And I hope they feel really sorry about it, too.

8.30am

Wa-hoooo! Dave the Rave is back – and he is just lovin' it!

9.00am

I said to Mum, 'Can we have another barbecue on Saturday? I want to invite Benny and Thomas.'

Mum said, 'Oh. Saturday … umm…'

I went on, 'Did you hear what I said? I said I want to invite Benny and Thomas.'

Mum said, 'Possibly not Saturday.'

I said (slowly and very clearly), 'But, <u>Benny and Thomas</u>? Doesn't that mean something?'

'Er … should it?'

'Well, yes! I'm inviting Thomas to a barbecue. That means I can't be jealous.'

'And that's lovely,' Mum said. 'No, really, I'm <u>very</u> pleased. It's just … possibly not Saturday.'

9.15am

Why is it parents are never satisfied? 'Sort yourself out,' Mum said yesterday. 'Stop the grumpy old face thing.' So, what have I done? I've sorted myself out and I know my face isn't grumpy because I checked it in the mirror before I went downstairs. And now she doesn't seem to care!

Not only that, but she won't tell me <u>why</u> we can't have a barbecue. I mean, if we're doing something on Saturday, why doesn't she just say? You know, 'No, Davey, we can't have a barbecue on Saturday because blah, blah, blah.' It's not difficult, is it?

I tell you what <u>is</u> difficult, though. Trying to invite your friends round so that your other friends can see you're not jealous.

9.30am

OK. Back to **THE PLAN** minus Step 1. Step 2 is still good: Ask Thomas if he'd like to join in fun run on Friday. That ought to do it.

9.35am

Unfortunately, Step 2 does involve ringing Benny.

9.40am

Of course Step 1, inviting Benny and Thomas to a barbecue, also involved ringing Benny, but at least I could have just talked to Benny. Then Benny could have done the inviting Thomas bit. If I'm asking Thomas if he wants to join in the fun run, that kind of means <u>I've</u> got to talk to him. Which wouldn't be so bad if I'd talked to him before, but I haven't.

10.00am

When I say Dave the Rave is back, he is so definitely back!

I rang Paul.

I said, 'You up for some funny running?'

He said, 'Yup. I can be in my shorts quicker than it takes Benny to eat a large portion of chips.'

(And that is quick.)

I rang John.

I said, 'You up for some funny running?'

He said, 'Ah. Problem.'

I said, 'What kind of a problem?'

He said, 'My shorts are in the dirty washing basket.'

I said, 'Well, wear something else.'

He said, 'No, that's all right. I'll get them out and wear them anyway.'

Nice.

OK. So then, when we're all running round the park, I'm just going to say ever so casually, 'You know what we should do? We should go round to Benny's and invite Thomas to do the fun run with us. Just because Benny doesn't want to do it doesn't mean Thomas won't.'

Then, of course, John and Paul will go, 'Wow! So you're not jealous of Thomas after all. Benny was so wrong and so were we.' Not only that, but I won't have to talk to Thomas on my own so it won't be so awkward. It's brilliant! Coolest plan I've come up with since I decided we ought to do last summer's charity cycle ride dressed as tomatoes.

11.30am

Step 2 went like a dream – until we ran round to Benny's and there was no one in.

I said, 'What is it with Benny? Why is he never home any more?'

'Probably out showing England to Thomas,' said Paul. 'That's what I'd want to do if I had someone from France staying.'

'What, the whole of England?' asked John.

'No, not the whole of it, obviously,' Paul replied, 'but as much of it as possible I'd have thought.'

'Well, what am I going to do?' I said. 'How can I invite Thomas to the fun run if he's not here?'

Paul said, 'You can phone him up.'

Awesome. Talking to him on my own. Back to square one.

11.40am

On the plus side, Paul did say he was glad I'd got over my problem with Thomas.

I said, 'I never had a problem with Thomas.'

Paul said, 'No, but … you know.'

I said, 'No, I don't know. I'm sorry, but the people with the problem are the ones telling me I had a problem. It's like I've been saying all along, I'm not jealous.'

In bed

Dad came in.

So did Mum.

They came in together.

They never come in together. I mean, this is not a big bedroom. It looks crowded when I'm in it.

Dad said, 'About Saturday.'

I said, 'Yeah?'

Mum said, 'I've talked it over with Dad and we both thought it'd be nice if you knew.'

'Knew what?'

'Well,' Dad said, 'we thought we'd go on a bit of a day trip.'

'A day trip?' I repeated. This didn't sound like the sort of announcement that needed two parents to be in my bedroom at the same time.

'Yes, a day trip,' Dad said. 'To the seaside.'

OK, I thought. Weirder than weird. It's not as if we've never been on a day trip to the seaside before.

'That sounds ... cool,' I said. 'So, where are we going?'

For some reason, Mum seemed to be grinning all over her face but looked as if she was trying desperately hard not to. She and Dad exchanged a glance. I'm telling you, this was getting wackier by the second.

'You say,' said Dad to Mum.

'No, you say,' giggled Mum to Dad.

There was a pause.

'Well,' I said, 'I suppose you could always just blindfold me and I'll find out when we get there.'

'Silly!' laughed Mum. 'We're going on a day trip to –'

'Devon!' they both announced together.

'Devon for the day?' I frowned. 'That's miles away.'

'It is a few,' said Dad. 'But you'll love it when we get there.'

10.00pm

Lord God, thank You for today, it was good. I know Mum said I should give my bad thoughts to You but, the truth is, I don't have any. Not about Thomas, and **THE PLAN** proves it. I've sorted it out by myself. I knew I wasn't jealous, but now it's official. Paul said so. And I don't even need to talk to You about it because I'm so cool with everything. Totally peaceful. Well, I <u>was</u> totally peaceful until Mum and Dad came in and started behaving like mysterious mystery people from the darkest mists of mysteriousness. I mean, what was that all about? Please bless them, dear Lord, and help them to be like normal parents again in the morning. Amen.

THURSDAY 17 AUGUST
After breakfast

I said to Mum, 'I'm just going to ring Benny and see if Thomas wants to do the fun run tomorrow evening.'

She said, 'What fun run tomorrow evening?'

I said, 'The one I've been going to do with John and Paul for the last two months since the posters went up all over Holly Hill.'

Mum said, 'Yes, but you can't do it tomorrow.'

I said, 'But it's <u>on</u> tomorrow. When else am I going to do it?'

Mum said, 'Well, you'll have to give it a miss. We're leaving for Devon at the crack of dawn on Saturday. You need an early night.'

'But I'm not having the barbecue so I have to do the fun run. It's all part of **THE PLAN**.'

'What plan?'

'My plan.'

'So, make a new plan. Bed tomorrow night. Early. We're going to the seaside.'

9.30am

John rang.

He said, 'Thought you'd like to know I've just seen Benny and Thomas and you'll never guess what they were doing?'

'What?' I said.

'Practising for the funny run.'

I blinked. 'What, both of them? But I thought Benny didn't want to do it.'

'I know. Well, he's doing it now. And you'll never guess what else?' John went on. 'They're entering as their own two-man team. They're going to try and do the whole three miles as a three-legged run – you know, with their legs tied together. I mean, wicked, or what? And you'll never guess what they're calling themselves? "Team BennyTom"! So now you don't have to bother about asking Thomas to join in. He's doing it anyway.'

9.45am

I can't believe it. Benny didn't want to do the run. When the posters first went up, I asked him and he told me so himself – 'I don't want to do it,' he said. He told me if he could run the whole thing dribbling a football that would be different, but I said I didn't know if that was allowed. I mean, he never suggested running on three legs with me. He never said we could be called '**Team BennyTom**'. Not that we would have been '**Team BennyTom**', of course, because we'd have been '**Team BennyDave**', but that's not the point. Benny's doing more stuff with that sort-of-cousin-but-not than he's ever done with me.

11.00am

I wouldn't do that run now if Benny came round and asked me to himself. What's the point? It's not as if anyone'll miss me. Least of all my ex-best friend, obviously.

11.05am

Team BennyTom. How pathetic is that?

In bed

Mum came in to say goodnight.

She said, 'Night night, Davey.'

I said, 'Yeah.'

She went out.

Two seconds later, she popped back in.

'You know, Davey,' she said, 'this could all be completely in my imagination, and do say if it is, in which case I'll tiptoe away without another word, but I can't help noticing that you don't seem to be yourself again. Is there something I should know? Because if there is I wish you'd tell me. Has it got anything to do with our trip to Devon? I mean, I know you wanted to do the fun run, but I think you'll enjoy the day in Devon so much more if you're not worn out from going to bed late the night before. In any case, there's bound to be another fun run. And if you're really desperate to do some running, I'm sure we'll be able to find you a beautiful, sandy beach to run along on Saturday. They have lots of them down where we're going …'

The thing about Mum is, she likes you to talk to her

when you're not happy, but actually being able to get a word in can sometimes be a real achievement. Just when you think she's finished, off she goes again, until you've both pretty much forgotten why she started talking in the first place …

Hang on, though … it's gone quiet. She's stopped.

I opened my mouth. I was all ready to speak …

Too late.

In Mum jumped again.

'You're not still bothered about Thomas, are you? I thought you'd managed to sort all that out. You seemed so much happier about things yesterday.'

I waited for more. Mum has been known to go on indefinitely.

But this time there was nothing. Just Mum, with her mouth surprisingly closed, sitting on my bed, looking at me. Which actually made me feel kind of uncomfortable.

That's when I sensed it. The **lump** in my throat. It was somehow making my eyes prickle. Before I could stop them, there were tears spilling down my face.

Just stay cool, I thought. Maybe Mum won't notice.

She did, though.

She couldn't not.

'Why has Benny chosen Thomas over me?' I blurted out. 'I don't get it, Thomas has only been here a few days. I asked Benny to do the fun run with me and he didn't want to. But now he's doing it with Thomas. They've got a team name and everything – Team BennyTom. I mean talk about stupid!'

I tried to laugh but all that came out was more tears.

'Come here, Softie,' Mum said, and gave me one of her super-special mega hugs. 'I'm sure this is all a silly misunderstanding. You and Benny, you're mates. Nothing's ever going to change that, I just know it.'

'But it's changed already,' I choked. 'And all because of that Thomas.'

Mum was quiet for a moment (_so_ not like her), then she asked, 'Did you do what I said the other day? Did you ask God to take the bad thoughts away?'

I shook my head and felt under my pillow for a tissue. There wasn't one but it didn't matter. Mum was already holding one out.

'I didn't have any bad thoughts,' I began, blotting my face. It felt hot and sticky. 'I was annoyed with Benny, that's all, and who wouldn't be? I mean, he did forget to come to my barbecue because he'd rather be out doing something with Thomas that didn't involve me. So anyway I thought, if I haven't got any bad thoughts, I can't give them to God because there's nothing _to_ give to God. And as it turned out I didn't need God to help me feel better anyway. I did it all by myself. I decided I could _prove_ I wasn't jealous by following **THE PLAN** – prove it to Topz and prove it to you. It started to work, too. You were all thinking you'd been wrong about me. And I _was_ – I really was feeling so much better, and then ...'

'And then what?'

'And then Benny decided to do the fun run with Thomas and leave me out all over again! **I hate that Thomas!**'

Mum was looking thoughtful. Then suddenly she got up, went round to the other side of my bed and picked up my Bible.

'Sometimes,' she said at last, 'we can get things a bit mixed up. We think that how our friends and family see

63

us is more important than how God sees us. It's easy to see why. No one wants their friends to think badly of them or tell them they could maybe have dealt with something a bit better. The trouble is that, although you thought you'd made it look as if you weren't feeling jealous any more, that was you just … well, pretending. It was a bit of a cover up. And it worked as far as we were concerned. For a while at least. We thought you'd sorted things out. But God isn't taken in so easily,' she went on. 'He sees through our cover-ups. We can pretend to the whole world and fool everybody. But the one we can't pretend to is God. He sees it all – good thoughts, bad thoughts, happy and sad thoughts. And although that may seem quite scary, it's actually pretty wonderful.'

Mum had been flicking through the Bible and now held it open at Psalm 139. I know that psalm really well. I just seemed to have forgotten it lately.

She didn't read the whole thing. A few verses, that's all, but they were enough:

'Lord, you have examined
me and you know me.
You know everything I do;
from far away you understand all
my thoughts …
you know all my actions.
Even before I speak,
you already know what I will say …
Examine me, O God, and know my mind;
test me, and discover my thoughts.
Find out if there is any evil in me
and guide me in the everlasting
way.'

Psalm 139
Psalm 139
Psalm 139
Psalm 139
Psalm 139
Psalm 139
Psalm 139
Psalm 139
Psalm 139
Psalm 139
Psalm 139
Psalm 139
Psalm 139
Psalm 139
Psalm 139

64

'You see,' she said. 'You don't need to prove anything to me or your dad or your friends because we love you. Everyone gets things wrong sometimes. I do, don't I? Look at that sweater I've knitted. I know it's awful. But you still love me, and no doubt so will your dad when I give it to him for Christmas.

'And when we get things wrong, God still loves us too. He just waits for us to own up to them and then come to Him and say sorry. If there's something going on inside you that's not quite right, covering it up won't hide it from God. He knows us better than we know ourselves, the Bible says so,' and with one finger, Mum tapped the verses she'd been reading. 'Whatever it is you're feeling, Davey, just give it to Him. And if you're not sure what it is, ask Him to show you. He will take it away. We need to let God in to deal with the things that make us unhappy and lead us to think bad thoughts. Otherwise we can end up just burying them – and burying them doesn't get rid of them. It means they'll come out again another time in another way. Just remember, however you feel, you're not on your own. You've got God on your side.'

When Mum went downstairs, she left the Bible open on the bed.

10.00pm

Only one thing to do, I reckon – write my own psalm:

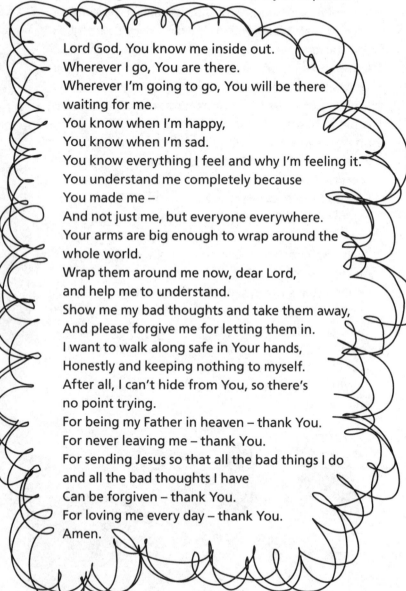

Lord God, You know me inside out.
Wherever I go, You are there.
Wherever I'm going to go, You will be there
waiting for me.
You know when I'm happy,
You know when I'm sad.
You know everything I feel and why I'm feeling it.
You understand me completely because
You made me –
And not just me, but everyone everywhere.
Your arms are big enough to wrap around the
whole world.
Wrap them around me now, dear Lord,
and help me to understand.
Show me my bad thoughts and take them away,
And please forgive me for letting them in.
I want to walk along safe in Your hands,
Honestly and keeping nothing to myself.
After all, I can't hide from You, so there's
no point trying.
For being my Father in heaven – thank You.
For never leaving me – thank You.
For sending Jesus so that all the bad things I do
and all the bad thoughts I have
Can be forgiven – thank You.
For loving me every day – thank You.
Amen.

FRIDAY 18 AUGUST

10.00am

Rang Paul and told him I wouldn't be able to make the fun run tonight.

He said, 'Why?'

I said, 'Mum's orders. Day trip to Devon tomorrow so I have to go to bed early.'

'That's rubbish,' he said. 'Not the day trip to Devon, which actually sounds pretty cool, but the early to bed bit. Shall I talk to your Mum? I know some almost guaranteed ways to get my own way with mine. They might work on yours.'

'<u>Almost</u> guaranteed?' I said.

'Yeah, you know,' he went on cheerfully. 'For example, I ask her things when she's trying to watch her favourite TV programme and doesn't want to have to think about much.'

'Does that really work, then?' I asked.

'Not often,' he sighed. 'Rarely really … in fact not at all. Looks like you're stuck with an early night, then.'

'Looks like I am.'

'Enjoy Devon.'

'Looks like I may as well.'

11.30am

Benny rang. Mum answered.

She called up, 'It's Benny.'

I said, 'For me?'

She said, 'Generally speaking, it is you Benny rings up to talk to.'

I said, 'I know, but …'

'But nothing,' Mum said. 'Now, are you going to come and take this phone because I'm getting a pain in the shoulder standing here holding it out for you?'

I took the phone.

'Hello?'

'Yo, Dave the Rave!'

'Er, yo, Benny the ... Benny.'

It was just as if nothing had happened; as if nothing had changed; as if nothing had gone wrong.

'What's this I hear about you pulling out of the fun run?' Benny asked.

'Not pulling out, exactly,' I hesitated. 'Just can't really go now. How did you know?'

'Saw Paul and John funny running at the park. Actually, me and Thomas were much funnier than they were. We kept falling over. We're trying to run three-legged.'

'I know,' I said. 'I mean, I heard. Team BennyTom.'

'Yup,' Benny went on. 'That was Thomas's idea. In fact the whole thing was Thomas's idea. I said I didn't want to do the fun run unless I could dribble a football and he said, "What if we do it on three legs?" – which actually sounded way cooler than dribbling a football.'

'Oh,' I said. 'I thought ... when John told me about your team and everything ... well, I thought ... I mean, the thing is, I asked you if you'd like to do the fun run and you said no, and so when I heard you were doing it with Thomas, I thought you'd ...'

'You thought I'd what?'

I couldn't say it. It sounded ridiculous even to me: 'Well, Benny, if you really want to know, I thought you'd chosen Thomas over me – again.' I mean, what was I thinking? Benny would never do something like that. Not deliberately. How could I have let myself even begin to have such crazy thoughts? Sometimes the massive

MASSIVENESS

with which I get things all wrong amazes me.

'You thought I'd what?' I heard Benny say again.

'Oh … nothing, really,' I mumbled.

'So anyway,' Benny said cheerfully, 'what I was going to ask you was if you'd like to come over after the fun run for a bit of a Topzy ice cream-making extravaganza, only Paul said you weren't doing it.'

'No,' I said, 'I can't. But, I mean, if I <u>was</u> doing it, an ice cream-making extravaganza at yours would have been awesome.'

'<u>Awesome</u> does not even begin to cover what it would have been!' whooped Benny. 'Stonkingly stonking, that's a bit closer – although maybe *tray, tray,* stonkingly *bonne* says it best.'

'How's the French going, by the way?' I asked.

'*Tray, tray, stonkingly bonne,*' he replied.

'And … how's Thomas?' I managed to say.

'He's great. You should come over. You'd really like him.'

'Yeah. Thanks. I know.'

'And Thomas would really like you, too. So,' finished Benny, 'come over when you get back from your day trip to Devon.'

'Yeah,' I nodded. (Don't know why I nodded when he can't see me.) 'Maybe I will.'

11.40am

'Everything all right?' Mum asked when I put the phone down.

'Yup,' I said, 'I think maybe so. Except that I'm going to miss out on an ice cream-making extravaganza tonight because I have to go to bed early.'

Mum winked at me. 'I'll buy you an ice cream by the sea to make up.'

I raised my eyebrows like Dad does when Mum gets him a different sort of breakfast cereal. Sometimes she thinks he ought to work on 'expanding his breakfast horizons' rather than being bogged down with porridge every morning.

'Just one?' I said. 'I think missing a Benny ice cream-making extravaganza has got to be worth more than a measly <u>one</u> ice cream.'

'<u>Don't</u> push your luck,' Mum said.

7.30pm

Thank You, Lord, that You always hear us when we talk to You. I know that's true because You've been hearing me ever since I gave my life to You, right here on this very spot of floor in my bedroom. (Well, I've had a new carpet since then, but the spot on the floor's the same.)

You never stop listening to me and guiding me. But sometimes, I stop hearing You when You're not saying what I want You to. I suppose it's when I think I'm right and the rest of the world, including You, is just SO wrong. I'm sorry for those times, Father God. I'm sorry for acting as if I know better than You do, or for thinking I can handle stuff all on my own.

And I'm sorry for the bad thoughts I've been having … and for being jealous.

There, I've said it. All that nastiness inside, it was jealousy – me being jealous of Thomas because I thought he'd stolen Benny. Please forgive me, Lord, and keep me talking to You – and listening to You – now and always. Amen.

SATURDAY 19 AUGUST
6.00am

It's hard to believe that we're up at the crack of dawn and Dad is still insisting on cooking porridge for breakfast.

Mum said, 'Why can't you have cornflakes just for this morning?'

Dad said, 'Because it's a long drive to Devon and I'll never get there on a bowl of cornflakes.'

'Well, have two bowls, then,' Mum said.

'If I'm going to spend time munching my way through two bowls of cornflakes,' Dad said, 'I may as well spend time making one bowl of porridge and eating that.'

6.30am

In the car, on the road, on our way. And guess what?
I get to be in charge of the digital camera!

6.45am
Day Trip To Devon – Part One

You see, I was talking to Paul yesterday and when I told him Dad had said I could have the camera for the day, he got really megaly excited and said, 'Ooh! Oooh! You could make a film and post it on YouTube! I mean, wow! You and your Devon adventure could become the latest must-see viewing … which would mean you could

become an enormous YouTube star ... which would mean you might not have time for Topz any more because you'll be spending so much time signing autographs and looking cool in bright-red sports cars!'

I said, 'Why would I be in bright-red sports cars?'

Paul said, 'For all the photos. When you're famous, you have to be seen in bright-red sports cars. Wearing sunglasses.'

So anyway, not that I'm posting anything on YouTube or anywhere else, but making a film is actually an awesome idea. Although when I told Mum she didn't think so.

'How can I relax if I've got a camera in my face all the time?' she complained.

I said, 'It won't be in your face all the time. Just some of it.'

She said, 'Yes, but it's bad enough having someone taking photos of me without having to look at myself on film as well.'

I said, 'You don't have to look at yourself. I'll only watch it when you're not in the room.'

She said, 'Yes, but if I know I'm on film then I'm going to want to see it, aren't I? I mean if everyone else has seen it, I certainly don't want to be the only one who hasn't.'

Dad said, 'I think a film's a great idea. We've got loads of photos, it's about time we did something different.'

'Really?' said Mum. 'And this from the man who will only ever eat porridge for breakfast.'

7.00am

So, like I say – **Day Trip To Devon (DTTD) – Part One**. Not hugely interesting at the moment, I must admit. I've got cars going by and the back of Mum and Dad's heads.

Paul says I have to do a commentary on what I'm filming.

I said, 'Why? Won't what I'm filming be obvious? I mean, I'll be filming it which means anyone watching will be able to see I've just filmed a tree, for example, without me having to say, "And here we have a tree".'

'That's not the point,' said Paul. 'This is a video log. The commentary is the really important bit – the bit that will help the viewer share the total experience of your day trip.'

I had no idea Paul knew so much about the technical wotsits of video logging.

So, anyway, here we have it. Dave the Rave's video log – my commentary on our DTTD – Part One:

It's amazing how many people are driving around at 7 o'clock on a Saturday morning. In the time it took to say that, five cars have whizzed by. And there go another three. Oh, and that's the back of Mum and Dad's heads. Hold on, Mum's saying something.

'David, put that thing away. Can't we at least wait until we get there before you start all this filming nonsense?'

You see, that's the trouble with grown-ups today. No sense of adventure.

8.00am

DTTD – Part Two

Just been trying to persuade Dad to stop at the next motorway services. He's not interested. Let's try again.

'Dad, can we please stop at the next motorway services?'

'What do you want to stop for?'

'What people normally stop for – leg stretching and snacks.'

'We've only been in the car for an hour and a half. Your legs can't need stretching yet.'

'They do, though.'

'Well, stretch them out on the back seat. And you wouldn't need a snack, either, if you'd had porridge for breakfast.'

Ooh. Did you see that? That was Mum giving Dad one of her 'looks'. I suppose it can't always be easy being married to someone who thinks porridge is the answer to whatever the question is.

9.00am

DTTD – Part Three

Finally, a travel stop. This is a very big car park …
There goes Dad, disappearing into the distance to get takeaway drinks. If my camera-work's looking a bit shaky it's because I'm having trouble unbending my legs, what with them having been bent in a sitting position for the last two and a half hours. Mum's obviously having trouble unbending hers, too.

'David, you're not filming this, are you?' (That's not one of her happy voices.)

'Filming what?'

'Me – stuck like this?'

'Only a bit. And anyway, no one will ever guess it's you. After all, you don't normally stand like that.'

9.30am
DTTD – Part Four

On the road again … Are we there, yet? … And just for you, Paul – Oh, look, there's a tree …

9.50am
DTTD – Part Five

Definitely in Devon now. I know this because, as you can see, there are lots of trees and hills and things, and if there's one thing Devon's got lots of, it's hills. It was also a bit of a clue when we passed a big road sign saying 'Welcome to DEVON'. Plus a few miles ago, Dad said, 'Here we are, then, in Devon.' Not much gets past me, you know.

10.45am
DTTD – Part Six

We've arrived! You may have noticed it's not very sunny. That doesn't seem to be stopping people walking around in their shorts and flip-flops, though.

   And there's an ice cream van!
   'Mum! There's an ice cream van.'
   'So?'
   'You said you'd buy me lots of ice creams.'
   'I said I'd buy you one ice cream.'
   'Well, one … lots … same difference.'

11.00am

DTTD – Part Seven

And there it is, viewing people – the sea. That twinkly blue stuff Devon's famous for. Not that it's that twinkly or blue today as the sun's decided to do a no-show. Still, it's not stopping the surfers. Take a look at all the surfing dudes surfing away out there. On surfboards. In the surf. I should have brought my surfboard … Hang on, I haven't got one.

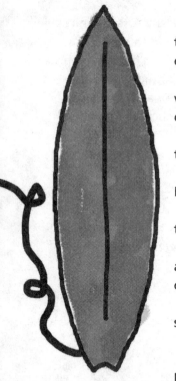

'Mum, can I have a surfboard?'

'David, do all our conversations today have to take place on camera?'

'Of course they do. It will help viewers share the total experience of our day trip.'

'How on earth did you manage to come up with that?'

'I didn't. Paul did. So anyway, can I have a surfboard?'

'Do you like the idea of living by the sea, then?'

I'm now pointing the camera at myself so that you can see my confused expression.

'Mum, I'm asking for a surfboard, not to move house.'

'Yes, of course. Absolutely.'

'What, yes, absolutely, I can have one?'

'Let's ask your father.'

As you've probably noticed, Dad is doing his impression of the Invisible Man at the moment. He was here and now he's gone. I asked Mum where he was when I first noticed he was missing and she said, 'Oh, he won't be long. You know what your dad's like.'

1.00pm
DTTD – Part Eight

And here we are in the car again, Dad having mysteriously reappeared.

'So, Dad, just so viewers understand why we're in the car driving around the streets of Devon rather than playing on the beach, which is presumably why most people come here, can you please explain what we're doing?'

'Well, I can't talk to the camera, can I, I'm driving.'

'That's OK, Dad. The side of your face is pretty much as perfect, if not more so, than the front.'

'Right, well, I just thought it would be good to … look at the whole area. Not all of Devon's beachy, you know.'

So, there you have it, viewers, not all of Devon is 'beachy'. There are actually houses here. Like the one we're looking at now.

'That's a lovely house, Dave.'

'Mum, it's just a house. Can we please go back to the beach?'

'Yes, Davey, but imagine being lucky enough to live there. You'd be able to go to the beach every day.'

'Actually, Dad, speaking of people who go to the beach every day, can I have a surfboard?'

2.00pm
DTTD – Part Nine

Just coming to the end of our picnic, but before I eat
the last of my sandwiches, I have to show you what's
inside. Look at that. This has to be one of Mum's best
ever, super-duper, scrummy-yumptious, gorgeously
fandabulous sandwich fillings – cream cheese, grated
carrot, sweetcorn and salad cream, topped off with a
sprinkle of crushed salt 'n' vinegar crisps. I mean, wicked
or what? I'm just going to show you the sea for a few
moments now while I eat … (That crunching sound,
that's not the sea, by the way. That's the salt 'n' vinegar
crisp bit of the sandwich.)

4.00pm
DTTD – Part Ten

Guess what I've been doing? Here are some clues: note
my wet-looking, sand-splattered legs, my soaking shorts
and my sticky-with-salt hair. You can probably also see
that I've gone vaguely purple. That would be because
I've been in the water and it's absolutely freezing.

4.10pm
DTTD – Part Eleven

OK, what you're about to see is unbelievably scary, so if
you don't want to be unbelievably scared, look away …
NOW.

'Dave, your dad's just going for a quick paddle.
There's no need to film him.'

'Oh, but there is.'

As you can see, viewing people, Dad has gone for the
rolled-up trouser look.

'Dad, why didn't you just wear your shorts?'

'Not really a shorts person, I suppose. Anyway, this works just as well. Going to come back in the sea?'

'Er … with you dressed like that? I think not.'

I mean, just look at those legs … Hope nobody's in the middle of eating …

6.30pm
DTTD – Part Twelve

This is my empty fish and chip plate. A few moments ago it was piled up with fish and chips and beans and mushy peas. I don't actually like mushy peas, but sometimes when you're by the sea it's necessary to go for the complete, full-on seaside fish and chip experience. Mind you, Dad also had a pickled egg, but I just couldn't bring myself to go that far. Actually, I couldn't even bring myself to film him eating it … bleeaaaah.

7.30pm
DTTD – Part Thirteen

One last look at the sea … Rather hilariously, Dad was planning for us to be on our way home half an hour ago, but he forgot where he parked the car. He he he he he.

'Stop that, David, it's not funny.'
'I can't, Mum, because it is.'
He he he he he he he!

11.45pm

DTTD – Last Part

Home to our little home. Which means this is the end of our Day Trip To Devon. All I can say is I hope you've enjoyed 'sharing the total experience', as Paul would say, as much as I've enjoyed sharing it with you.

'Mum. Dad. Say goodnight.'

'Actually, Dave, would you like to turn the camera off now, please. Your dad's got something to say.'

'Say away, then.'

'But this is sort of a family only thing.'

'Mum, catching family only thing sort of stuff on film is good. It's all part of the viewing enjoyment. It's what'll make us such a big hit on YouTube.'

Dad's actually looking quite serious now. Much more so than when he had his trouser legs rolled up – which, generally speaking, made him look extremely funny.

'Did you enjoy today, Dave?'

'I did, Dad, it was cool. Mega cool. In fact, ice cool when I went in the sea.'

'And what do you think of Devon?'

'It's good. Maybe next time we go I can get a surfboard.'

'Maybe next time we go you can. You're certainly going to end up with plenty of opportunity to go surfing if you want to.'

'What's that supposed to mean? What is this?'

'We're both just really pleased you had a great time because what this is, Dave, is that, um …

'we're moving, We're going to live in Devon.'

SUNDAY 20 AUGUST

7.00am

'What this is, Dave, is that, um … we're moving. We're going to live in Devon.'

I've been watching Dad saying that in the tiny little camera screen. I've watched him over and over again. At least a hundred times. But however many times I hear the words and look at him as they come out of his mouth, it doesn't make them sound any better. I keep trying to spot a twinkle in Dad's eye or work out if he's trying to stop himself bursting out laughing. I keep waiting for him to say, 'Only joking.' Not that that would be possible on the end of the Day Trip To Devon film because the moment he said the words, 'We're going to live in Devon', the battery in the camera died and everything went off. I had to charge it up overnight.

But the thing is, he didn't say, 'Only joking' off camera either. He and Mum just sort of gave each other a giggly little nudge and went on about how much they'd been dying to tell me but wanted to save the surprise until we got back home.

'Are you surprised, Davey?' Mum had asked.

I must have been staring at her quite blankly because after that she said really quickly, 'D'you know, you look absolutely exhausted. Come on, hop into bed and we'll talk about this more in the morning.'

Sometimes I think parents must live in a crazy, unreal sort of world all of their own that has nothing whatsoever to do with the world their children live in.

Don't they know me at all?

Did they really think I'd be able to get to sleep after that?

81

7.30am

Just been in to Mum and Dad. They were both still asleep so I thought I'd sit on the end of their bed until they woke up. When it didn't look as if they were going to wake up for ages, I thought I'd help them. By pretending to sneeze.

Very loudly.

Dad grunted and Mum sat bolt upright.

achoooo

'Dave, what ...? What do you think you're doing?'

'That's what I wanted to ask you. I don't want to move to Devon.'

Mum flopped down again.

'Come on, it's going to be wonderful,' she yawned. 'You enjoyed it there yesterday, didn't you? I know it sounds like a big step but we are going to have so much fun. Sand, sea and ice cream, not to mention your very own surfboard. What more could a young chap like you want?'

'I enjoyed it for the day,' I muttered. 'I'd even enjoy it for a holiday. But I don't want to live there. All my friends are here. My school is here. My **LIFE** is here. Why do we have to go somewhere else?'

Dad sighed. 'It's because of my job,' he said. 'I'm being transferred to the Devon office. I've been having meetings with my bosses but ... if I don't go, Dave, then I won't have a job any more.'

'But there must be loads of other things you could do here,' I said. 'Just get a new job.'

Dad shook his head. 'I'm afraid it's not that easy. Anyway, I met my new boss yesterday. She seems very nice. That's where I disappeared off to when you thought I'd turned into the Invisible Man. I just didn't want to say anything to you until I was absolutely sure what was going on. Well, now I am, and the thing is, if I've got to be transferred somewhere, there are far worse places than Devon. It's fantastic there. You're going to have a brilliant time. And the first thing we're going to do is get you that surfboard.'

'But I love Holly Hill. It's my home. I never want to live anywhere else.'

'I love it, too,' said Dad. He looked upset then, I thought. 'So does your mum. It's just that sometimes things have to change. We may not want them to, but if it's got to happen, we have to try and follow them through.' He paused. 'God's got a plan for all this, Dave, I know He has. We may not be able to see the whole picture yet, but bit by bit He'll show us what's going on.'

'Why not think of this as an adventure?' suggested Mum. 'Everyone likes adventures.'

'Not me,' I said. '**I hate them.**'

'Dave, this isn't easy for any of us, you know,' said Mum. 'Although, to be honest, I'd love to have lived by the sea when I was your age. And you'll be able to have the Topzies to stay. Just think of all those barbecues on the beach.'

'But they won't want to come and stay, will they? If I'm not living here any more, they'll forget all about me. I won't still be a part of the Gang.'

That's when I remembered Dad driving us round different houses.

'Is that where we're going to live? In that house you said was lovely?'

'We don't know where we're going to live yet,' said Mum. 'We were just having a little look round, that's all. Nothing like that's been decided yet.'

'Good,' I said, 'because whatever house you're thinking of moving to, you can count me out. I'm staying in Holly Hill.'

8.00am
Rang Benny.

I said, 'I really need to talk to you. I mean really, really.'

'Cool. Because I really, really need to talk to you, too,' said Benny. 'Only not now because we're about to go.'

'Go where?' I asked. 'Aren't you going to church?'

'Not this morning, but probably tonight. We're off to the safari park now. Dad's had a few days off but he has to go back to work tomorrow so he wanted to show Thomas the lions and dolphins today. D'you know what? Thomas has never seen a real dolphin before. And guess what else? Actually don't bother guessing because it is just so out-of-this-worldy stonking that you never will. Thomas and his family – well, not definitely or anything, but they might be going to move to England from France. Here – to Holly Hill!'

8.05am
Don't remember much else. I think Benny may have said, 'How was Devon? No, tell me later. I really have to go.' And that was that.

8.15am
I really need to talk to my best friend and I can't because of Thomas. Thomas who's always in the way.

Thomas who's moving to Holly Hill. **Thomas who's stolen my life.**

9.00am

Mum's just called me down for breakfast. Can you believe that? My world has just dropped into the deepest, boggiest bottomless pit of miserableness, and Mum wants me to go and eat something.

9.45am

Paul rang.

He said, 'Did you get to Devon all right?'

I said, 'Yup.'

He said, 'Did you get it all on film?'

I said, 'Yup.'

He said, 'Are you coming to church?'

I said, 'Yup.'

He said, 'Can you bring it with you so we can have a look?'

I said, 'Nope.'

He said, 'Why not?'

I said, 'Because I've deleted it.'

It's gone. Forever. Every last little bit.

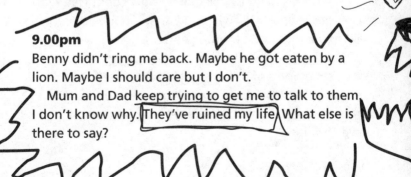

9.00pm

Benny didn't ring me back. Maybe he got eaten by a lion. Maybe I should care but I don't.

Mum and Dad keep trying to get me to talk to them. I don't know why. They've ruined my life. What else is there to say?

In bed

Lord God, why have You done this to us? Why does everything have to change? Why is Thomas allowed to be here when I have to go? Have we done something to annoy You? If we have, then I'm really, really sorry. Please put everything back like it was. I just want to be able to stay in Holly Hill. Amen.

MONDAY 21 AUGUST

9.30am

Danny rang.

He said, 'Are you coming to the meeting this morning?'

I said, 'What meeting?'

He said, 'At Greg's. To make Robin Hood costumes for the carnival.'

I said, 'I'm not doing the carnival. I wanted to be a pirate.'

Danny said, 'Oh, come on, Dave. I reckon you could be the snazziest merry man on the float. Please be there. We can always do pirates next year.'

It wasn't his fault. Danny didn't know about Dad's job because I hadn't told anyone. At Sunday Club I'd hardly said two words. But I shouted at him anyway.

'What's the point of doing pirates <u>next year?</u> What's the point of doing <u>anything</u> **NEXT YEAR?** I'm not going to be here, am I? I'm moving away. Not that any of you lot will care because by then you'll have Thomas!'

3.00pm

Sarah rang.

'Are you really moving away?' she asked.

'Looks like it,' I answered.

'But that's awful,' Sarah said. 'Do you have to?'

'Yes. Apparently I do.'

'But … will we ever see you again?'

'Dunno. Anyway, got to go.'

I don't actually have to go anywhere. I've just got nothing to say.

3.15pm

Paul rang.

He said, 'This is a joke, right?'

I said, 'What?'

He said, 'The moving away thing?'

I said, 'Paul, if you think that's me being funny, your sense of humour must be even weirder than I thought it was.'

3.25pm

Josie rang,

'Is it true?' she said. 'Are you moving away?'

'Yup,' I said.

'When?' she asked.

'Dunno,' I said.

'Will we be able to come and visit?'

'Dunno. If you want to.'

'Of course we'll want to. Why wouldn't we want to?'

'Dunno. Maybe because you'll have Thomas. I'm moving out. He's moving in.'

'He might not, though,' said Josie. 'Anyway, what difference does that make? We're still going to miss you.'

'Oh,' I said.

Pause. Then –

'Please do the carnival,' Josie said. 'It won't be the same if you're not there.'

3.35pm

Benny rang.

He said, 'Have you been on the phone all afternoon? Every time I try and ring you, you're talking to someone else.'

I said, 'It's not my fault if people want to talk to me.'

He said, 'So anyway, what's this about you moving away?'

I said, 'I'm moving away. That's about it, really.'

He said, 'Is that what you wanted to talk to me about yesterday?'

I said, 'Yup, but you were busy.'

He said, 'Sorry. We were on our way out. It's just a bit difficult with Thomas here.'

I said, 'I know.'

He said, 'D'you want to come over now? We could talk about it when you get here.'

I said, 'No thanks. Nothing to say.'

'There is, though. There's everything to say. Like how much you just can't leave Holly Hill because what will happen to Topz without Dave the Rave?'

'Topz'll be fine and I have to leave because apparently that's just the way it is. In any case, you'll have Thomas.'

'So?' Benny said. 'Thomas might be Thomas, but you're Dave the Rave and Topz won't be Topz without you.'

3.45pm

I want to believe Benny. I really do. But somehow …
I just can't.

TUESDAY 22 AUGUST

8.00am

Sometimes I don't feel in control of anything. Not even
my own space in my own house in my own bedroom.
I knew Greg had rung. I knew he was talking about
me with Mum. She was on the phone to him for ages
yesterday. What I didn't
expect was for him to knock
on my door in the evening and
walk in holding a merry man
costume.

'Hope it's OK to come on
up,' Greg said. 'Your mum said
it was.'

That figures. My parents
seem to make all the decisions
about my life these days.

Greg said, 'We made you a merry man outfit. At
least, Benny and Thomas did – although instead of
"Robin Hood and his Merry Men", we're actually calling
the float "Robin Hood and the Sherwood Foresters"
because there are going to be girls, too. So, strictly
speaking, this is a Sherwood Forester outfit. I know it's
not a pirate, but everyone would really, really like you
to join in with them.'

I nodded.

Greg said, 'I was chatting to your mum about you
having to move away. She says you're very upset.'

I shrugged. Why were we even talking about this?

Greg couldn't change anything – unless, of course, he could give Dad a new job.

'It probably won't make it any easier,' he went on, 'but did you know your parents are actually very upset, too?'

He waited, but I didn't answer. I don't really care what Mum and Dad are feeling. They're the ones making all the decisions. I'm just the one who has to go along with everything.

'Can I sit down?' Greg asked.

I didn't want him to but I shuffled along the bed to make room.

'Sometimes,' he said, 'things happen that we don't like and we don't always understand why. But even if we can't work the situation out, what we have to do is give it to God day by day, and then try and trust that He'll look after us and make something good come out of it.'

'That's easy for you to say,' I mumbled. 'You're not the one whose life's just dropped into a bottomless pit of ... bottomlessness.'

'That's true,' nodded Greg. 'But this isn't easy for any of us, either – not me, not Sunday Club, not Topz. Have you any idea how much we're all going to miss

you? Sarah was in tears yesterday when Danny told us.'

'Really?' I somehow wasn't expecting that.

'Really,' Greg replied. 'We all love you to bits. But even if you have to leave us, God is never going to let go of you. Whatever you do and wherever you go, He'll be right beside you.'

I screwed up my face. I had to. It was the only way I could stop myself from crying.

'But everything's gone **wrong!** My life's all **ruined** now. Where's God in that?'

'Talk to Him,' Greg said. 'Tell Him how you're feeling. You could even ask Him to help you understand. He knows we get confused and disappointed by things. All He asks us to do is to keep trusting Him; to keep believing that whatever happens, He will hold us in the palm of His hand. He will <u>never</u> leave us.

'And one more thing. Don't be too hard on your mum and dad. It can be tough for parents, you know. It's no easy job being responsible for everything all the time, especially when something big happens. They're the ones left with having to try and make the right decisions for the whole family. Your mum and dad love you so much. It might not seem like it, but when they decided you'd all have to move away, they were thinking of you, too. Your dad's in a difficult situation because he needs a job. I know you're confused and it's all a bit of a shock but … be kind to them.'

8.30am
Been reading my Bible. Just before he went home, Greg gave me a verse to look up. Luke 6 verse 37:

'Do not judge others, and God will not judge you; do not condemn others, and God will not condemn you; forgive others, and God will forgive you.'

8.45am

Dear Lord God, I've been so angry about moving – with Mum and Dad. With You. I don't understand why this has to happen, but then I don't think Mum and Dad do either. I've been acting as if it's all their fault and it's not. I've been blaming them when it's hard for them, too. Please forgive me for judging them and, just like Greg says – just like You want – help me to be kind to them instead. I suppose everyone needs kindness and understanding – even parents.

And Lord, if there's any way we can possibly stay here and not have to move, I pray that You will find it for us. But if it turns out that we just have to go then … please help me accept that, too. Help us all accept it. In Jesus' name I ask this. Amen.

9.00am

I think that's the most grown-up prayer I've ever prayed.

9.30am

'All right?' Mum said when I went downstairs.

'I'm sorry, Mum,' I just about managed to mumble. 'I know it's not your and Dad's fault.'

I'm not sure, but I think Mum was trying not to cry, too.

'Thank you, Davey,' she gulped. 'It's going to be all right, you know. One way or another. You, me, your dad – we're going to be fine.'

'I know. You, me, Dad … and God.'

'All for one and one for all?'

No idea what that means but, 'Sure. Definitely,' I said.

All for one and one for all   All for one and one for all   All for one and one for all
All for one and one for all   All for one and one for all   All for one and one for all
All for one and one for all   All for one and one for all
All for one and one for all   All for one and one for all   All for one and one for all
All for one and one for all   All for one and one for all   All for one and one for all
All for one and one for all   All for one and one for all   All for one and one for all

92

THURSDAY 24 AUGUST

10.00am

Mum said, 'What are you up to today?'

I said, 'Building the carnival float with the Gang. Well, I say "the Gang". It'll be the Gang plus Thomas.'

Mum said, 'That's all right though, isn't it?'

'Why wouldn't it be?' I said. 'I mean, Thomas will be in the Gang one day when he lives here, and I won't be when I don't.'

'You'll always be in the Gang,' Mum said. 'Friends like you've got don't just drop friends like you, simply because they can't be around all the time any more.'

'Yes,' I said, 'but if there's someone new in the Gang, it won't be the same. So not being around all the time won't matter.'

I went to grab my shoes, but Mum said, 'Hang on a minute.'

I said, 'I've got to go. I have to help put up a tree in Sherwood Forest.'

Mum said, 'But everything's OK now, isn't it? You're not feeling bad about Thomas again?'

'Why would I be?' I said. 'He's who he is and I'm who I am. There isn't room in the Gang for both of us. So if he's coming to live here, it's a good job I'm moving on.'

7.00pm

Awesome tree. Not a real tree, that is. We've borrowed it from the local theatre group, the Holly Hill Players. It's made of wood like a real tree, but with painted on leaves rather than naturally growing ones. We're calling it the miracle tree. You see, it gets used every year in the Holly Hill pantomime, and because the Players perform in the community centre, it's usually stored away in one of the sheds round the back that got flattened in the thunder storm. So it should actually have been squished to a pancake. But only the day before the storm, Mr Pickard, who's one of the Players, had taken it home to give it a new coat of paint. How mega is that?

Greg put me and Thomas in charge of putting the miracle tree together. It's in four pieces and does up with bolts. Bit of a fiddle but, like Mr Pickard says, there aren't many places you can easily store a fake tree unless it comes apart.

I said to Greg, 'No, that's OK. Thomas can do it with Benny.' I mean, come on, I was thinking, Thomas and me, we've never even spoken to each other.

'Nope,' said Greg. 'I've got Benny on the list to go to the garden centre for bamboo canes.'

I said, 'Did they have bamboo in Sherwood Forest?'

He said, 'No. But we need something to look like arrows to put in the quivers we're going to be carrying.'

John said, 'What's a quiver?'

Paul said, 'It's what a merry man puts his arrows in.'

John said, 'But why's it called a quiver?'

'Dunno,' Paul shrugged. 'Maybe seeing all those arrows makes people start quivering.'

That was the moment Benny went all jelly-like and started wibble-wobbling round the hall, going, 'Let's all quiver, wooooo!'

I glanced at Thomas.

'So,' I said, 'have you got used to Benny yet?'

'Not sure,' Thomas said. 'Does anyone ever get used to Benny?'

'Good point,' I said. 'What do you think is his most

unforgettable feature?'

'The amount he eats,' Thomas said. 'Definitely.'

8.00pm
The worst thing about Thomas is ... I actually really like him.

9.00pm
Mum and Dad have been on the Internet looking for houses in Devon.

Dad said, 'How was the float-building?'

I said, '**Cool**. I put a tree together. How was the house-hunting?'

Dad said, '**Cool**. I reckon we'll find something really nice.'

I said, '**Cool**.'

'Yeah,' Dad said. '**Cool**.'

9.30pm
Benny rang. And you know what? I really wish he hadn't.

FRIDAY 25 AUGUST
5.00pm
Mum said, 'You're very quiet today.'

I said, 'No, I'm not.'

She said, 'Dave, it's nearly time for Dad to get home and so far today all you've said is, "Yes", "No", and "Maybe, but without the cabbage".'

I said, 'Well, what's wrong with that? Nobody feels chatty all the time, which is a good thing. If you were chatty all the time, you'd probably end up losing your voice because it would wear out. Then you wouldn't be able to be chatty even on the days when you really wanted to be.'

In bed

How could Benny say that to me? When he rang yesterday, how could he possibly think it was OK to say that?

'Yo, Dave,' he said. 'We are going to have such a stonking float.'

'I know,' I said.

'Did you like the arrows?' he said.

'Loved them,' I said. 'Although I'm glad it wasn't me sticking all those feathers in the top of the bamboo.'

'They look wicked though, don't they?' he said. 'Almost like the real thing, Thomas reckons. And he should know – what with being a proper archery-type person and all that. Which reminds me, Thomas is why I'm phoning.'

'Why's that, then?' I asked.

'Well, we were talking about you moving and saying how it is SO not cool that you have to leave, especially as Thomas might be coming to live here now, and then Thomas had this totally stonkingly awesome idea. D'you want to hear it?'

I suppose the fact Benny told me is my fault really, because I said yes.

'You see, Thomas thought,' Benny announced unbelievably gleefully, 'that when you move out, maybe he and his family can move into your house!'

'What?' I said. For a minute, what he was saying didn't actually sink in.

'Yeah!' shrieked Benny. 'Is that a great idea, or is that a massively **GREATISSIMUS** idea? That'll

mean that when you come to visit from Devon, you'll
still be able to go into your old house, because even
though it won't be your house any more, it'll still be a
Topz house.'

'A Topz house?' I mumbled.

'Yeah,' said Benny. 'Obviously when Thomas comes to
live here he'll be a proper Topz, instead of being a sort
of "visiting-only" type of Topz which is what he is at
the moment.'

11.00pm
You see? Now it's official. Benny's sort-of-cousin-but-
not has <u>officially</u> stolen my life.

SUNDAY 27 AUGUST
1.30pm
At Sunday Club, Benny said, 'If I didn't know better,
Dave, I'd think you were avoiding Thomas and me.'

I said, 'And I wonder why I'd be doing that?'

Benny said, 'How am I supposed to know? You seem
to have stopped talking to me – again. What's up?'

I said, 'Benny, if you have to ask, it's not even worth
explaining it to you.'

4.30pm
Been cycle racing in the park with Danny and Josie.
It was great to start with. I was like a mad, cycling
wasp buzzing along. Josie says I must have turbo-
charged knees.

She said, 'You'll be able to cycle along the beach
when you live in Devon.'

Danny said, 'You probably can't cycle along the beach
because you'd gradually sink in the sand.'

Josie said, 'How do you know? Have you ever tried it?'

Danny said, 'Well, no, but I mean you're bound to, aren't you? Sand's sinky.'

'I think you're forgetting,' Josie said, 'how lightning fast Dave is on his bike. He wouldn't have time to sink.'

I'm going to miss Josie tons when we move. Everything she says makes so much sense.

But then, of course, something had to come along and spoil everything – the 'something' being Benny and Thomas.

'Hey, guys!' called Benny. He was wheeling his bike. 'Here comes Team BennyTom. We're going to do some time trials if you want to join in.'

Danny looked at me, then, 'Er, that's OK,' he said. 'We'll just carry on racing.'

'I tell you what,' said Benny, 'any chance we could borrow a bike for a minute? Thomas reckons he could beat me if we're both cycling flat out and he is **SO wrong.**' He paused. I wasn't going to look at him, even though I knew he was looking at me.

'Dave?' Benny asked. 'It'll only be for a sec. That's all it's going to take for me to prove who's the hare-brain and who's the tortoise-face.'

Sometimes these days I think that ending up knowing Benny has got to be the worst thing that has ever happened to me. Has he got no idea how bad I'm feeling right now – how bad he's made me feel? But then, of course he hasn't. He's been so busy with his new best friend, he hasn't even bothered to ask.

I ripped off my cycle helmet and threw it on the ground.

'Here!' I hissed, dropping my bike with a crash beside it. 'It's all yours. Thomas wants it, Thomas can have it. After all, he's having my house. He may as well have my bike, too.'

I ran off.

I heard Josie calling after me, 'Dave, wait!'

There was no way I was sticking around. Not for anyone.

5.00pm

Mum says she and Dad have found a lovely house. She's very excited because it's got a downstairs toilet.

I said, 'Mum, only you could get excited about having a downstairs toilet.'

She said, 'Nonsense. I know people who'd give just about anything for a downstairs toilet.'

'That is true,' agreed Dad. 'You may find it hard to believe, Dave, but a downstairs toilet can make the difference between buying a house and not buying a house.'

Sometimes I'm convinced Mum and Dad really belong in some weird parallel universe and only ended up in my world by accident.

5.30pm

Doorbell went. I looked out of the window. It was Benny and Thomas. They'd brought my bike home.

If Josie thinks I can cycle fast, she should have seen how quickly I dived into the shower.

'Dave!' Mum called up. 'It's Benny and Thomas. They've brought your bike back.'

'Sorry?' I pretended not to hear.

'Benny and Thomas are here. They've brought your bike back.'

'Sorry, I can't hear you. I'm in the shower.'

6.00pm

On second thoughts, a downstairs toilet is actually a pretty brilliant thing. It means you'd be able to lock yourself away in the upstairs bathroom for hours on end without ever having to come out.

In bed

Mum said, 'Benny told me to tell you he's sorry. He said you'd know what he was talking about.'

'OK,' I said.

'Do you want to tell me what he was talking about?' Mum asked.

'Nothing to tell,' I said.

'I know Thomas might be moving to Holly Hill,' Mum said. 'Is that what this is about?'

I shrugged.

'Because the point is, Dave,' she went on, 'whatever new things are going to happen for Thomas, that doesn't change the fact that new things are going to happen for you, too. And Jesus is going to walk with you every step of the way. That's what matters.'

10.00pm

You know what? In actual fact, moving away might be the best thing for everybody. It's like I say, the Topz

Gang's not big enough for me <u>and</u> Thomas. So if there's a good time to leave, it's got to be now.

BANK HOLIDAY MONDAY 28 AUGUST

11.30am
Paul rang.

He said, 'What're you doing?'

I said, 'Packing.'

He said, 'Why? Where are you going?'

I said, 'Duh. I'm moving house.'

He said, 'What? Today?'

I said, 'No, not today.'

He said, 'Then why are you packing now?'

I said, 'Because you need to be prepared for these things. Besides, it's not as if I'm doing anything else.'

He said, 'Aha! That's where you are completely wrong and inside out in a hedge backwards.'

'And in English that would be …?'

'You're coming camping at my house,' Paul said. 'Grab your tent.'

'When?' I asked.

'Tomorrow night.'

'Sounds awesome,' I said. 'It's just … is this a Topz camp-out?'

'What else could it possibly be?' Paul said.

'No,' I said, 'I mean is it just Topz? Only Topz? As in no one else but Topz?'

'Topz exclusivissimo,' Paul announced.

'Groovy,' I said. 'See you there.'

11.35am

Wickedissimus.

Knew I could count on Paul to be exclusive.

2.00pm

Mum said, 'David, why have you put all your clothes in
black plastic sacks?'

'Why do you think?' I asked. 'Because we're moving.'

'Yes, but we're not moving yet. We haven't even put
our house up for sale, let alone found another one.'

'Ah yes,' I said, 'but when the time comes, I'm going
to be ready.'

'Well, that's lovely and everything,' said Mum, 'and
I really appreciate you being so helpful, but it might
be an idea to hang on until everything's … well …
finalised.'

'But what's to finalise?' I said.

'Just hang on for a bit,' Mum said. 'There's no point
living out of black bags.'

2.15pm

If we're going to go, let's just go, that's what I say.
I guess I'm going to have to stop packing, though. I've
run out of plastic sacks.

TUESDAY 29 AUGUST

3.00pm

Just had to unpack half my clothes so there were some
bags free to put my camping stuff in.

I said to Mum, 'Can't we just buy some more?'

She said, 'No. We're not moving yet. You can put your

clothes back in the cupboard and use the bags we've got.'

Just you wait, though. When the time comes to go to Devon, who'll be the first one to be in trouble for not being packed? Me, obviously. There is just no pleasing some people. Parents in particular. Mums particularly in particular.

6.00pm
Dad's dropping me off at Paul's in a minute with all my gear. This is going to be great. Better than that, it's going to be stongkingly groovy, because Thomas will not be anywhere in sight. He may be going to take over my life at some point in the near or far future, but he's not in Topz yet, and Paul said this is a

TOPZ EXCLUSIVISSIMO

camp-out. So if Benny's there he won't be with Thomas and we might even possibly maybe share a tent. How triffy-trick is that? Tonight's going to be just like old times.

WEDNESDAY 30 AUGUST
6.00am
I think sometimes you imagine something's going to be a certain way because you want it to be like that so much. I SO wanted Paul's camp-out to be brilliant. I so wanted it to be like <u>the</u> **BIG** Topz event of the summer. Just the snazzy seven – me, Benny, Sarah, John, Josie, Paul and Danny. Something I could remember when the time came to move away. I wanted to feel Topzy again.

Only that's not what happened. Not remotely.

Everyone hates me. Every single Topz.

And why wouldn't they? I hate myself.

6.15am

I was the first one there. As soon as Danny and Josie arrived with the other tents, we had a competition to see who could put them up the fastest – me and Danny versus Paul and Josie. Danny and me won the first time. Then, on the second time, we almost had ours finished when I got my foot caught in one of the ropes, lost my balance and fell over – slap on top of the tent we were putting up. It sort of flopped sideways onto the grass, so we had to start all over again.

When he managed to stop laughing for long enough, Danny spluttered, 'Why couldn't you fall the other way?'

'I had my foot caught,' I answered. 'In a foot-caught-in-a-tent-rope situation it's not that easy to choose which tent you're going to land on.'

'Doesn't bother us,' grinned Josie. 'In fact it gives us a chance to do this!' And she banged in the last peg.

'Our tent is up! Winners!' shrieked Paul, and he did this mad kind of abominable snowman-type dance around the garden – at least that's what I imagine an abominable snowman would look like if he was dancing. Although, probably without the glasses.

So we ended up with a tie, although as Danny said, we would have won by miles if I hadn't decided to sit on our tent.

As soon as John and Sarah arrived, Paul's dad lit up the barbecue. I say, 'barbecue', but  because this is Paul's dad we're talking about, this was no ordinary barbecue like you might buy down at the garden centre. This was a super-duper, ultra cool, built-by-hand, 'Paul's dad special' type barbecue. He'd made it himself out of bricks and it was awesome.

'Wow!' I said.

'Glad you like it,' he smiled. 'Any time you'd like me to throw one together in your garden, just say the word. I'd love it.'

'That's true,' said Paul. 'If there's any chance of a spot of do-it-yourself, Dad will be right there in the thick of it. In fact, you daren't stand still too long in our house or you might find he's started to turn you into a bookcase.'

'Thanks,' I said, 'but our garden's not going to be our garden for much longer, so there wouldn't be much point in your building us a barbecue. Anyway,' I added, 'when's Benny getting here?'

'Soon, I think,' Paul said. 'He was out doing something with Thomas today so whenever they're back, I suppose.'

Stonking, I thought. Because why wouldn't I think that?

Only what I should actually have thought was, 'Hopefully they won't get back for ages and then it'll be too late for Benny to come over; hopefully when it comes to it, Benny won't be in the mood for a camp-out; maybe he'll think he'll have missed all the

food so he might as well stay at home.
If only he'd stayed at home …'

But none of that happened.

What happened was this.

Benny turned up when I was half-way
through my third burger. Those burgers were
so good – homemade by Paul's mum just like
the barbecue was homemade by Paul's dad.

I saw Benny step out of the back door.
When I waved at him I managed to flick
tomato sauce all across my T-shirt. I glanced
down to wipe it off, then looked back up all
ready for Benny to grin and say something
Benny-ish like, 'Dave, have you still not
worked out where your mouth is?' – and
that's when I saw him; standing next to
Benny as if he owned the place; standing
next to Benny as though they'd been friends
forever; as though they'd <u>be</u> friends forever
now because I'd be well and truly gone.

<u>That's when I realised
Thomas was there, too.</u>

I didn't go over. I couldn't
finish my burger. Suddenly
it felt as if I was holding a
lump of concrete.

'All right, Dave?' said
Danny.

'Yeah,' I grunted. 'Why
wouldn't I be?'

'I don't know, you just
look a bit … funny.'

'I'm fine,' I said. 'Actually, I don't think I can eat any more. I'm going to find a bin.'

I headed for the kitchen. Benny and Thomas were by the barbecue now. I had to get away from them; get out of the garden.

Paul's mum was at the kitchen table, slicing open some more burger buns.

'Burgers all right for you are they, Dave?' she asked.

'Y-yes,' I mumbled. 'They're lovely.' I looked at the soggy remains in my hand. 'Sorry, I've just got a bit … full up.'

'I know what you mean, they are a bit stodgy, aren't they?' she smiled. 'There's a bin over by the sink.'

'Thanks,' I nodded and went over to it. My eyes were stinging. I was going to cry, I just knew it. Paul's mum must have known it, too.

'What's the matter, sweetheart?' she asked. 'Has something happened?'

I shook my head. 'No, I'm fine, it's just … you know … onions frying …'

Whether she believed me or not I'm still not sure but she said, 'I know, dreadful, aren't they? Tell you what, you go in the other room for a minute. I'll get Paul to bring you in a cold flannel. There's nothing stops your eyes smarting like a cold flannel, I always think.'

And before I could say, 'No, that's OK, actually I think I might just go home', she'd bustled off.

I went into the front room and sat on the sofa. Paul was there like a shot.

'What is it?' he said. 'Mum said it might be onions, but on the other hand it might not be. Are you crying?'

I shook my head. I couldn't speak. The last thing I was going to do was cry in front of Paul.

'Dave, what is it?' He plonked down on the sofa next to me. 'You were all right a minute ago. What's happened?'

'What's happened?' I gulped finally. 'As if you don't know.'

'I don't actually,' he shrugged, 'that's why I asked.'

I took in a deep breath. 'You said this was a

Topz exclusivissimo *camp-out.'*

'Yeah,' said Paul. 'So?'

'I can't believe I've got to spell it out!' I hissed. 'If it's Topz exclusivissimo – what in the whole wide universe is Thomas doing here?'

Paul frowned. 'He's with Benny.'

'But you never said Thomas was invited,' I snapped. 'Just Topz, you said, and Thomas **ISN'T TOPZ.'**

Paul sat there staring at me for a moment, as if he couldn't quite make me out … as if he didn't really know me somehow.

'Dave,' he said in the end, 'I don't know what's going on with you, but Thomas is on holiday with Benny. That means where Benny goes, at the moment Thomas does too. And I may have said "Topz exclusiv … iss … imo" (although if I did I'm quite surprised because that's not an easy word to get your tongue around) but anyway that wasn't supposed to mean that no one else was allowed. We might be a gang but Thomas is part of that for now.'

'Yes, but it's not just "for now", is it?' I said. 'He's probably going to live in Holly Hill. When I move away, he's probably going to live in my house! Ever since he came here, all he's been trying to do is take over.'

'No, he hasn't,' Paul answered. 'He's been joining in, that's all. And you know what? I'm glad. His mum's been really ill and if he's been able to have a bit of fun while he's here, then that's got to be good.'

'Yeah,' I said, 'and about the whole "his mum's been really ill" thing. If _my_ mum was really ill, the last thing I'd do is leave her behind while I went away on holiday!'

6.45am

I keep thinking about something Greg said when Thomas hadn't been here very long: 'Don't let your angry thoughts lead you into doing angry things.' I told myself I didn't know what he meant, but really I think I did. It's just that I was _so_ angry with Thomas for coming to stay with Benny and making the holidays different from how I thought they'd be – and I wanted to stay angry with him. I know I asked God to help me stop feeling jealous, but when I found out we were moving away and Thomas was moving in, it all came back. That's when I should have thought about what Greg said. That's when I should have given it to God all over again.

Only I didn't.

Instead I got angrier and angrier.

Until I somehow didn't seem to care who I shouted at or who I hurt.

angry angry angry angry angry angry angry angry angry angryangry angryangry angry angry

7.00am

Sometimes you see things that I think maybe you never forget. I know I'm never going to forget Thomas's face when I said what I said to Paul: 'If _my_ mum was really ill, the last thing I'd do is leave her behind while I went away on holiday!'

109

Thomas was standing in the doorway. Neither of us saw him until it was too late. He'd heard everything and there was nothing I could do. I couldn't un-say it. I couldn't make it right. For a split second, I wasn't even sure that I wanted to.

Thomas just sort of stared at me, blinking. And then he was gone.

Paul chased after him, but he shot out of the front door so fast there was no hope of catching up. Then by the time everyone else knew he'd run off, there was no sign of him.

I just remember all the questions:

'What happened?'

'Did he say where he was going?'

'Why would he run off?'

'Has he got a mobile phone?'

'He won't have gone far, will he?'

And then worst of all –

'Did you say something, Dave? What did you say?'

I don't know why Paul was so kind. I didn't deserve 'kind'. I deserved horrible – like me.

'It doesn't matter what got said,' Paul answered quietly. 'All that matters is that we find Thomas.'

Paul's mum rang Benny's parents to ask if he'd gone back there, but they hadn't seen him. So Benny's dad came round straight away and joined in the hunt, while his mum stayed in the flat in case he turned up. He'd been in Holly Hill long enough to be able to find his way there on his own now.

Then everyone went off in two groups. It was

beginning to get dark, so no one was allowed to go out by themselves. Benny's dad took Benny, John and Sarah, and Paul's dad went with Paul, Danny and Josie.

Just as he was leaving, Benny looked straight at me and said, 'Aren't you coming?'

I dropped my eyes. I couldn't even look back at him.

Suddenly I felt Paul's mum's hand on my shoulder.

'I don't think Dave's feeling very well, are you, Dave?' she said. 'Probably best if I ring home and someone comes and picks you up.'

I never realised before. Paul's mum is as kind as he is.

Out of the corner of my eye, I saw Benny shaking his head. And then there was just me and Paul's mum standing in the hallway. The search parties had gone.

'I don't know the whole story here,' she said, 'but I know some of it. Paul's a proper old chatterbox when he gets going. He's been a bit worried about you for a while, you know. It'll be all right. Thomas won't be far away. They'll find him.'

'But it's all my fault,' I murmured. 'He could be anywhere and it's all my fault.'

'Tell you what, then,' she said, 'why don't we go and have a little look? Just you and me together?'

I shook my head. 'No point. I'm the last person he's going to want to see.'

'In a way,' she said, 'I think you could be the very best person for him to see. And, looking at your face, I think he's probably the very best person for you to see right now, too.'

If this was my mum, I could have argued. But it was Paul's mum so I couldn't say a word.

We turned left up the road and went towards the shopping centre. Paul's mum said there'd be no point going to the park because the others would be sure to cover every square inch of it. It was bound to be one of the first places they'd look. She said we'd be better off going the other way.

We didn't talk much. All I kept thinking was, 'Thomas must be so scared.' He didn't know Holly Hill very well. He didn't know England very well. He'd run away because of what I'd said and I don't even know what made me say it. It was just like Greg had tried to tell me. Angry thoughts lead to doing angry things. They'd led me to say the cruellest words I've ever said. Now Thomas was lost and on his own. Because of me.

I started to pray. I'm not sure when, I just suddenly found myself saying, 'Lord God, please look after Thomas, please keep him safe until we find him' – over and over again, like that. Deep inside my head.

And then I saw him. We hadn't even got as far as the shops. When all the other Topz were out looking, I don't know why it should have been me. I don't know why I was the one to find him.

I nudged Paul's mum and pointed. 'There!'

Thomas was standing at a bus stop on the other side of the road, peering at the timetable.

We came up behind him. Paul's mum stayed a little way away. She had her phone out. I guess she was ringing Paul's dad to call off the search.

'Hi,' I said.

When Thomas turned round, he looked half surprised.

'What are you doing here?' he asked.

'What d'you think we're doing here?' I said. It wasn't easy looking at him. He'd been crying and his eyes were dark and empty somehow.

'I … er …' I began, 'I just needed to let you know … I'm sorry. I didn't mean to say what I said. I don't even know what made me say it.'

Thomas shook his head. 'No,' he said, 'you were right. Mum wanted me to come here but I should have said no. She's not well, I should have stayed with her. So I'm going to go home now.'

'What, on the bus?' I said. 'You won't get all the way to France on the bus.'

'I know,' he said, 'but I'll get some of the way.'

'You see, the thing is,' I said, 'actually, what I was hoping … what we're all hoping … is that you'll just come back to Paul's.'

'That's right,' said Paul's mum. She was standing beside me now. 'Paul will be ever so upset if he doesn't get to say goodbye. And Benny will be. So will all the others. Besides, you coming here has been good for your mum. She's been able to have a rest, knowing you're safe with your friends having a lovely holiday. If I wasn't very well, that's just what I'd want for my Paul.'

Thomas didn't say anything and he certainly didn't look convinced.

Paul's mum added, 'Come back for tonight, eh? It's a bit late to be going anywhere now. Then, in the morning, if you still want to go home, it can all be arranged properly.'

After a moment or two, Thomas nodded. Then Paul's mum put an arm round him and we started to make our way back.

But the closer we got, the worse I felt. I may have been the one to find Thomas. I may have said sorry. But how could I walk into Paul's house and face all of Topz now?

'Actually,' I said, 'I think I'm going to go home.'

I was near enough. It would only take me a few minutes from where we were.

'Oh, please come back with us,' said Paul's mum. 'You haven't had any strawberries and ice cream yet.'

'That's all right, thanks,' I said. 'I kind of want to be on my own anyway.'

'Well, you're not walking by yourself in the dark. We'll come with you to the gate.'

Just before they left, I told Thomas I was sorry again. I told him how it wasn't anything he'd done, it was just how I was feeling. Holly Hill, Topz, barmy Benny – that was my life. I didn't like change. I didn't like things being different from the way they had been; the way I thought they always would be … and I didn't want to have to move away. I'd been jealous and then I'd got angry. And I was just really, really sorry.

SORRY SORRY SORRY

8.00am

Lord God, it all started with a niggle. Just one tiny niggle in my head that got bigger and bigger until I let it take over. I wasn't thinking about You. I wasn't thinking about Thomas. All I cared about was how **I've** been feeling; how everything's been affecting **me**. I've been so unfair. So selfish. Please forgive me, Lord. I don't know what else to say except I'm sorry. Amen.

SORRY SORRY

10.00am

Mum's been in to see me.

'Are you coming out of your room or are you just going to hide away in there all day?' she said.

'I'm going to hide away in here all day.'

'That's a shame,' she replied. 'Can I hide away with you, then?'

'Mum,' I said, 'the idea of hiding away is to be on your own.'

'Yes,' she went on, 'but if you're on your own, you can't talk about things. And if you can't talk about things, you can't sort them out. And if you can't sort them out, you just stay sad. And if you just stay sad, well ... you just stay sad.'

'But there's nothing to sort out. I'm horrible so Thomas ran away. That's about it, really.'

'You may have <u>said</u> something horrible,' Mum smiled, 'but that doesn't mean you <u>are</u> horrible.'

'I pushed Thomas out. I did everything I could to make him feel he wasn't wanted here.'

'So?' Mum said. 'We all do the wrong thing sometimes, you know. There can be all sorts of reasons for it, too. Let's face it, things haven't been exactly easy for you lately, have they?'

'That's not an excuse, though, is it, Mum? Jesus accepted everyone all the time. It didn't matter how He was feeling, He included everyone, never left anyone out. And that's what He wants us to do, too. That's the way He wants us to live. I've let Him down.'

Next thing I knew, Mum was sitting on the floor next to me. That was quite a surprise actually. She doesn't like sitting on the floor. Whenever she comes into my room and finds me slouched out on the rug, she always goes on about me having 'a chair and a bed, the perfect places to park myself, and what do I do, I sit on the floor'.

'We all let Jesus down,' Mum said. 'We can't help it. That's why we need Him. That's why He came to earth. For that very reason – so that whenever we do something wrong, we have the chance to say we're sorry and be close to God again.' She shifted her position. 'So, if you've said sorry to God and meant it, which I know you do, and you've said sorry to Thomas, which I know you are, then what's stopping you getting out there and being Topzy again?'

'I can't,' I shrugged. 'After last night, I just can't. In fact, after last night, I just want to get on with moving away.'

'Um, yes,' Mum said. 'About that.'

'<u>What</u> about it?'

'Well, it's just … oh, never mind.'

4.00pm

Paul rang.

He said, 'What're you doing?'

I said, 'Nothing much. What're <u>you</u> doing?'

He said, 'I'm ringing you.'

I said, 'Oh.'

He said, 'Thomas is OK, you know. He even had strawberries and ice cream when he got back in last night. He's spoken to his mum and he's going to stay on until Sunday.'

'Great,' I said.

'He's still going to be in the carnival on Friday evening. Robin Hood and his merry band of Sherwood Foresters are all ready to go.'

'Cool,' I said.

'So what we're all hoping,' he went on, 'is that you're going to be on the float with us.'

To be honest, that was the last thing I thought Paul would say. To be even more honest, it was the last thing I wanted. Not because it was Robin Hood instead of pirates but because, after everything that had happened, I just couldn't face it.

'Thanks,' I said. 'I mean, really, thanks. I didn't expect anyone still to be talking to me, let alone inviting me to do stuff.'

'You'll come then?' said Paul.

'No,' I said. 'No, I won't.'

4.15pm

Not doing the carnival is good practice for moving away. After all, this time next year, I won't be here to do it anyway, so I may as well get used to it now.

7.00pm

When Dad came in from work, he was whistling. I haven't heard him whistling for ages.

THURSDAY 31 AUGUST

4.00pm

Paul rang.

'You're definitely not doing the carnival tomorrow, then?' he asked.

'Definitely not,' I said.

'Because, the thing is, we're short of a bucket shaker,' he said.

'A what?' I said.

'A bucket shaker. Someone who can walk beside the float shaking a bucket under people's noses for them to put money in so we can raise enough for the new plants at the community centre.'

'But there are loads of you,' I said. 'There must be someone who can do it.'

'Nope,' said Paul. 'Everyone's too busy being part of the Sherwood Forest scene. At the moment, the only bucket shaker is Greg and that's just not enough.'

'Well, I –'

'So, you'll do it, then?'

'No, I –'

'I'm telling you, there is literally **NOBODY** else. So what's it going to be? Yes or no?'

5.00pm
Just tried on my Sherwood Forester outfit. It's not like being a pirate, but hey ho and shiver-me-timbers. Looks like I'm in the carnival.

In bed
Mum and Dad came in to say goodnight. Together. It made me very nervous. It's not that long since the last time they both came in together and look where that ended up – with me having to move to Devon.

'Glad you're going to be in the carnival,' said Dad.

'Me, too,' said Mum. 'We'll be there as you go past, cheering like idiots.'

That I can well believe.

'So,' said Dad, 'how are you feeling about the Devon move now?'

'Dunno,' I said. 'It'll be fine.'

'Uh huh, and what if,' Dad continued, 'I told you that maybe I'd been a bit hasty? Maybe I hadn't thought about things enough, and in particular about how moving might affect you?'

I wasn't sure what to say. I looked from Dad to Mum then back to Dad.

'What's going on?' I said.

'When I found out we'd have to move or I could end up without a job,' Dad began slowly, 'I panicked. I thought, right, let's just get on with it then. What I didn't do was pray. I didn't give God a chance to have His say.'

He paused. It probably wasn't for very long, but it seemed like forever.

'And?' I said.

'I suppose,' Dad went on, 'I never realised how important your home here is to you. So, when I saw how upset you were, that's when I began to wonder if I'd made a mistake.'

I could feel my heart beating faster and faster as he was talking. There was another pause and I hardly dared ask.

'And, what did you decide?' I mumbled.

'It's not so much what I decided,' said Dad, 'as what I've been doing.'

He'd stopped talking again. This was getting exasperating.

'Which is?' I prompted – exasperatedly.

'I've been praying, and the more I talked to God about moving, the more I wasn't convinced it was the

119

right thing to do. In the end I said to Him, "Lord, if you want us to stay here, You're just going to have to show me by finding me another job."'

He stopped again. How anyone could stop so many times in the same conversation is beyond me.

'Then what happened?' I blurted out.

Dad smiled and glanced at Mum. 'Well, amazing as it may seem in only a few days … I have just been offered another job,' he said. 'Looks like we're staying in Holly Hill.'

9.45pm

Wow. I'm shaking all over. I can hardly write. Just when I thought everything had gone about as wrong as could be … God's turned it all around.

10.00pm

Greg said to us at Sunday Club once that being a Christian is the most exciting adventure we'll ever have. He said, if we put ourselves in God's hands and allow Him to lead us, He'll take us on the most incredible journey.

Greg's right, isn't he? I asked God to help me accept having to move away and I think I sort of had, even though I still didn't want to go. But I also asked Him whether, if there was any way we could stay, He would find it for us. And He has. God's found my dad another job.

I guess that must mean that, for now, Holly Hill is exactly where He wants us to be.

10.15pm

Thank You so much, Lord God, that even though we make mistakes and get things wrong and let You down, You still have this perfect plan for each one of us. Thank You that although we can get into such a muddle trying to work something out, when we hand it over to You and invite You to work it out for us, You say, 'No problem, all you had to do was ask.' And thank You that, for now at least, Holly Hill is a part of Your plan for me and for Mum and for Dad. And when You do want us to move on, please help me to be ready.

Knowing You is **SO awesome!** Bring on the adventure ... Amen.

FRIDAY 1 SEPTEMBER
3.30pm

Getting dead nervous now. Paul's coming to call for me and we're walking down to church together to meet everyone at the float. We're using a big, flat trailer and we're being towed by a tractor! How cool is that! Last year we had the back bit of a truck but this is going to be way better. Paul says I don't have to be a bucket rattler the whole time so I get to ride on the float for a bit, too.

Only thing is it's the first time I'll have seen everyone since the camp-out. Paul's the only Topz I've talked to. He says, don't be daft and they're all looking forward to having me in Sherwood Forest, but I'm not so sure. Supposing I get there and it's obvious no one wants to know? I haven't told anyone we're not moving. I'll just wait for the right time ... and if there isn't a right time ... I won't say anything at all.

10.00pm

Sometimes, you have a moment that you just know
will last forever in the history of your most stonking
moments. There were certainly a few really good ones
this afternoon. Like when Benny, Thomas, Josie, Sarah,
Danny and John cheered their heads off as Paul and I
arrived at the float; and when the tractor joined the
procession, and the miracle tree began to rumble along
the road; and when so many people threw coins into
the buckets as we passed by that, by the end of the
evening, we'd raised enough money not only for all the
new community centre plants, but also for a bench so
that people could sit there and enjoy them.

But the best, by far the best thing that happened,
was just before the float set off when Thomas came
up to me and said, 'Thanks for coming to find me the
other night. Don't know where I'd have ended up if you
hadn't. The bus I was going to get on wasn't even going
in the right direction. Look, I've no idea at the moment
whether I'm going to be moving to Holly Hill. We have
to wait and see how Mum gets on. All I really want for
now is that you and me … can we just be OK?'

I was grinning all over my Sherwood Forester face.
Somehow or other, this was working out better than I
ever thought it could … No. Not 'somehow or other'.
This was God working everything out better than I ever
thought He could.

'You bet we can be OK, because I'm really, really sorry
for everything,' I burbled. 'We can be triple OK times a
million.'

'Stonking,' said Thomas. (He's definitely been
spending too much time with Benny.) 'Because,' he
went on, 'we thought it would be really triffic if we all

wore one of these.'

He pulled something out of his pocket. For a minute, I had no idea what it was. Then he put it on – and I could hardly believe it.

It was an eye patch. A pirate's black eye patch!

Suddenly I realised that they'd all put one on – all of Topz – and Thomas was holding another one out for me.

'Well,' he said, 'seems only fair. Robin Hood and the Sherwood Foresters is good, but Robin Hood and the Sherwood Forest Pirates is just SO much better!'

Collect the set:

Know God's help every day
Gruff and Saucy's Topz-turvy Tales
ISBN: 978-1-85345-553-7

Confidently step out in faith
Danny's Daring Days
ISBN: 978-1-85345-502-5

Become a stronger person
John's Jam-packed Jottings
ISBN: 978-1-85345-503-2

Keep your friendships strong
Paul's Potty Pages
ISBN: 978-1-85345-456-1

You can show God's love to others
Josie's Jazzy Journal
ISBN: 978-1-85345-457-8

Christians needn't be boring
Benny's Barmy Bits
ISBN: 978-1-85345-431-8

You are special to God
Sarah's Secret Scribblings
ISBN: 978-1-85345-432-5

£5.99 each

IF YOU LIKED THIS BOOK, YOU'LL LOVE THESE:

TOPZ

An exciting, day-by-day look at the Bible for children aged from 7 to 11. As well as simple prayers and Bible readings every day, each issue includes word games, puzzles, cartoons and contributions from readers. Fun and colourful, *Topz* helps children get to know God.
ISSN: 0967-1307
£2.49 each (bimonthly)
£13.80 UK annual subscription (6 issues, includes p&p)

TOPZ FOR NEW CHRISTIANS

Thirty days of Bible notes to help 7- to 11-year-olds find faith in Jesus and have fun exploring their new life with Him.
ISBN: 978-1-85345-104-1
£2.49

TOPZ GUIDE TO THE BIBLE

A guide offering exciting and stimulating ways for 7- to 11- year-olds to become familiar with God's Word. With a blend of colourful illustrations, cartoons and lively writing, this is the perfect way to encourage children to get to know their Bibles.
ISBN: 978-1-85345-313-7
£2.99

National Distributors

UK: (and countries not listed below)
CWR, Waverley Abbey House, Waverley Lane, Farnham, Surrey GU9 8EP.
Tel: (01252) 784700 Outside UK (44) 1252 784700 Email: mail@cwr.org.uk

AUSTRALIA: KI Entertainment, Unit 21 317-321 Woodpark Road, Smithfield,
New South Wales 2164. Tel: 1 800 850 777 Fax: 02 9604 3699
Email: sales@kientertainment.com.au

CANADA: David C Cook Distribution Canada, PO Box 98, 55 Woodslee Avenue,
Paris, Ontario N3L 3E5. Tel: 1800 263 2664 Email: swansons@cook.ca

GHANA: Challenge Enterprises of Ghana, PO Box 5723, Accra.
Tel: (021) 222437/223249 Fax: (021) 226227 Email: ceg@africaonline.com.gh

HONG KONG: Cross Communications Ltd, 1/F, 562A Nathan Road, Kowloon.
Tel: 2780 1188 Fax: 2770 6229 Email: cross@crosshk.com

INDIA: Crystal Communications, 10-3-18/4/1, East Marredpalli,
Secunderabad – 500026, Andhra Pradesh. Tel/Fax: (040) 27737145
Email: crystal_edwj@rediffmail.com

KENYA: Keswick Books and Gifts Ltd, PO Box 10242-00400, Nairobi.
Tel: (254) 20 312639/3870125 Email: keswick@swiftkenya.com

MALAYSIA: Salvation Book Centre (M) Sdn Bhd, 23 Jalan SS 2/64, 47300
Petaling Jaya, Selangor. Tel: (03) 78766411/78766797
Fax: (03) 78757066/78756360 Email: info@salvationbookcentre.com

Canaanland, No. 25 Jalan PJU 1A/41B, NZX Commercial Centre, Ara Jaya,
47301 Petaling Jaya, Selangor. Tel: (03) 7885 0540/1/2 Fax: (03) 7885 0545
Email: info@canaanland.com.my

NEW ZEALAND: KI Entertainment, Unit 21 317-321 Woodpark Road, Smithfield,
New South Wales 2164, Australia. Tel: 0 800 850 777 Fax: +612 9604 3699
Email: sales@kientertainment.com.au

NIGERIA: FBFM, Helen Baugh House, 96 St Finbarr's College Road, Akoka,
Lagos. Tel: (01) 7747429/4700218/825775/827264 Email: fbfm@hyperia.com

PHILIPPINES: OMF Literature Inc, 776 Boni Avenue, Mandaluyong City.
Tel: (02) 531 2183 Fax: (02) 531 1960 Email: gloadlaon@omflit.com

SINGAPORE: Alby Commercial Enterprises Pte Ltd, 95 Kallang Avenue #04-00,
AIS Industrial Building, 339420. Tel: (65) 629 27238 Fax: (65) 629 27235
Email: marketing@alby.com.sg

SOUTH AFRICA: Struik Christian Books, 80 MacKenzie Street, PO Box 1144,
Cape Town 8000. Tel: (021) 462 4360 Fax: (021) 461 3612
Email: info@struikchristianmedia.co.za

SRI LANKA: Christombu Publications (Pvt) Ltd, Bartleet House,
65 Braybrooke Place, Colombo 2. Tel: (9411) 2421073/2447665
Email: dhanad@bartleet.com

USA: David C Cook Distribution Canada, PO Box 98, 55 Woodslee Avenue, Paris,
Ontario N3L 3E5, Canada. Tel: 1800 263 2664 Email: swansons@cook.ca

CWR is a Registered Charity – Number 294387
CWR is a Limited Company registered in England – Registration Number 1990308